PRAISE FOR YOUNG KNIGHTS OF THE ROUND TABLE: THE KING'S RANSOM

"In a literary world rife with paranormal characters and situations, *The King's Ransom* offers a refreshing and realistic approach to pre-teen medieval reading material. [Each of] [t]he three young protagonists...faces his own fears with determination in the quest to solve the mystery, a journey filled with danger and suspense, and, ultimately, a highly satisfying conclusion...in this tale of coming of age. Cheryl Carpinello has written a clean, tight read without using any of the props so prevalent in the young reader's genre."

—Lela Buchanan, *Readers' Favorite Review*

"True to the legends of King Arthur, *The King's Ransom* sets the stage for grand adventure and includes many of the core elements present in other Arthurian tales, including honor, loyalty and friendship. Cheryl Carpinello's knowledge of medieval history is apparent in this timeless classic, which is rich in historical realism and is as enlightening as it is entertaining. Carpinello's telling of this heroic tale is sure to introduce young and even reluctant readers to the joy of reading. *Young Knights of the Round Table: The King's Ransom* is a literary treasure and earns the Literary Classics Seal of Approval."

—*Literary Classics Book Reviews & Awards*

"This is an entertaining and exciting Middle Grade read - a mystery, a quest and a trio of unlikely friends who make a pact to solve a murder in order to prove the innocence of the man accused of the crime - a man whose identity comes as something of a surprise at the end of the book."

—Wendy Leighton-Porter, author of *The Shadows From the Past* series.

"...[A] very well written Arthurian book for middle grade readers that I thought was perfect for readers of this age. Set in Wales in old castle Pembroke, the story follows three friends, Gavin, Bryan and Philip who get together to free their friend, The Wild man, who has been accused of murder and stealing a relic, a jewel known as the King's Ransom. Great book, I would recommend to all young readers!"

—CM Gray, author of the *Shadowland* series.

"*The King's Ransom* is a very enjoyable read. In the time of King Arthur, a young prince, a blacksmith's apprentice, and an orphan boy with a secret join together to find a stolen jewel (the "ransom" of the title) and save their friend, a mysterious hermit known only as 'The Wild Man'. Each has their own quest to fulfill to achieve their destiny. And they wind up solving not just one mystery, but three... The characters are fully realized, the story is well written and flows nicely. There's a good balance between action and dialogue, both internal and external. And I like the author's focus on the ideals of knighthood--it should appeal to all children, but especially to boys (who often seem to be forgotten these days)"

—Eric Tanafon, *Amazon reviewer*

"Pull out those swords and slide into your armor - can one slide into something that bulky? - Doesn't matter because this story will still feed the fantasy of children (especially boys), who dream of the days of knighthood...The characters were enjoyable and exactly as young knights should be, not perfect but not naughty; they definitely have their hearts in a noble direction. I loved that they are willing to risk all to save a friend, a cause kids will cheer for. Of course, the upbeat action, evil advisory, sword fights, secret-tunnels and witch make the story even more appealing. Yep, all those things that make the medieval world so exciting. I found the writing very fitting to the time period without falling into the trap of feeling too heavy or boring. The settings were described well, letting the reader fall into the time period."

—Dr. S. Drecker, *Amazon Reviewer*

BOOKS IN THE TALES AND LEGENDS FOR RELUCTANT READERS SERIES

Guinevere: On the Eve of Legend, Book 1 (Lexile Level: 750L)

Guinevere: At the Dawn of Legend, Book 2 (Lexile Level: 750L)

The King's Ransom, Young Knights of the Round Table
(Lexile Level: 720L)

Sons of the Sphinx (Lexile Level: 620L HL)

Tutankhamen Speaks (Lexile Level: 840L)

SHORT STORIES

Guardian of a Princess & Other Shorts

EARLY READERS

*Grandma/Grandpa's Tales: Wild Creatures in my Neighborhood
and What If I Went to the Circus*

*Grandma/Grandpa's Tales 2: Singers of Songs and
The Not Too Stubborn Humpback Whale*

AWARDS

2014 Gold Award Winner for Juvenile Fiction from
Global eBook Awards.

2013 EVVY Finalist and EVVY Merit Award forJuvenile/Young
Adult from Colorado Independent Publishers Assoc.

2013 Ariana Cover Finalist

2012 Silver Award Recipient for YA Fiction from Children's Literary
Classics and the CLC's 2012 Seal of Approval.

2012 Finalist E-Book Children from USA

2012 Best Book Awards

*To Connor —
Do you
have their
courage?,
Cheryl*

YOUNG KNIGHTS OF THE ROUND TABLE:

THE KING'S RANSOM

Cheryl Carpinello

Silver Quill Publishing

Young Knights of the Round Table: The King's Ransom

© 2012 by Cheryl Carpinello

Third Edition
Published in Print and eBook format by Silver Quill Publishing, 2019
Published in the USA
Sketches by: Jodi Carpinello
Map by: Cameron Carpinello
Cover by: Berge Design
Typeset and eBook Production by: www.typesettingbook.com

Lexile Level: 720L
Printed in the USA
ISBN: 978-1-912513-44-4 (Print)
978-1-912513-45-1 (eBook)

To Don, my husband and soul mate.
Thanks for believing.

Acknowledgements

Many thanks to 5th grader Cameron Carpinello for drawing the map.

I would like to thank Shelley Hegge's 6th grade students of 2010 for consenting to read and comment on the final draft of Young Knights. I promised them that I would list them by name, so here goes: Gunilla D., Mitch L., Tori M., Danielle N., Logan P., Jacob S., Hailey W., and Clara Y.

Thanks, Shelley Hegge, for once again letting me invade your classroom to road-test my work.

Special thanks to my reading colleague Louise Guillaudeu for her careful reading and insightful suggestions from the beginning to the end of this story.

Thanks to Marti Kanna of New Leaf Editing for taking the time to do the initial editing. Hopefully you see the product of your careful work in this final copy.

Thanks to Lea and the Muse editors for their willingness to give Young Knights a try and publish it first in EBook in 2012.

Finally, thanks to Bublish, Inc for helping to take my books to the next level.

TABLE OF CONTENTS

Map of Wales 1

List of Characters 2

The Contract 4

1   Gavin 10

2   The Thief 16

3   Philip 26

4   Bryan 36

5   The Knight's Vow 42

6   Spying 46

7   The Witch 54

8   The Decision 62

9   Gavin's Quest 68

10 Ghost of Manorbier Castle 78

11 Philip's Quest 88

12 St. David's Head 94

13 Bryan's Quest 100

14 Cardigan Bay Showdown 106

15 Quest Completed 112

16 A Secret Unveiled 122

17 Another Secret Revealed 130

18 And Then, Tom 138

More About Places Mentioned 141

About the Author 144

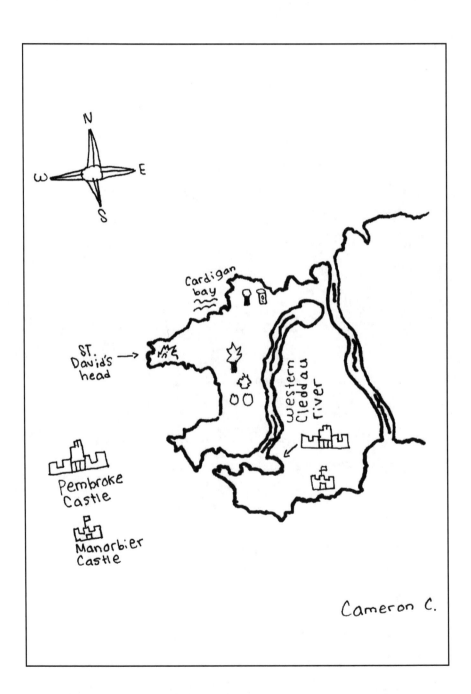

LIST OF CHARACTERS

Aldred: Estate manager for the castle and trusted treasurer.

Bryan Balyard: A blacksmith apprentice (15 years old) at Pembroke Castle.

Dunham: Once a knight of the King of Scotland, now an outlaw for hire.

Gavin: Youngest son (11 years old) of King Wallace the king of Pembroke Castle.

King Arthur: As himself.

King Edward: Monarch of Manorbier Castle, considers King Wallace an enemy.

King Wallace: Monarch of Pembroke Castle, father of Gavin, Robert, and Sean.

Philip: An orphan (13 years old) who mysteriously showed up at the castle.

Queen Katherine: Mother of Gavin, Robert, and Sean.

Robert: Gavin's oldest brother.

Sean: Gavin's older brother but younger than Robert

Tom: An urchin who lives at Manorbier Castle.

Wild Man, The: A beggar who came the castle one day and stayed; befriended Gavin, Bryan, and Philip.

THE CONTRACT

As the small weather-beaten boat plowed through the breakers, the man standing on the bow swayed with the motion. His scarred hands tightened on the rail. His cloak's hood blew off revealing his damp brown hair.

Dunham's gaze traveled up the massive granite cliff ahead and stopped at the site of the castle on top. The cold grey stones did not invite visitors, much like their king. It was a surprise when he received the letter offering him employment. Because he was an outlaw, work did not often seek him out. He was considered beyond the pale, not trustworthy. Once a trusted knight of a Scottish king, he had been caught stealing and was punished. Now his left hand carried the brand that marked him a thief.

Jumping off the boat, Dunham entered the doorway cut into the granite wall as he was instructed. The rock swallowed him up as his black cloak blended with the darkness. He cursed as his boot slipped on a moss-covered rock.

"Sire?"

"Yes, what is it?"

"The man you are expecting is making his way through the Smuggler's Pathway."

"And the boat?"

"It has left the shore and is headed back out to sea."

"Good. Escort him here when he emerges from the pathway. And have one of the kitchen maids bring in another jar of ale when he leaves."

"Yes, Sire." The servant backed out of the throne room and left.

"Finally, I can put my plans into motion," King Edward of Manorbier Castle said out loud, his voice echoing off the stone walls. He hobbled over to the chair to hide his disfigurement from his impending guest.

Emerging from the tunnel, Dunham spotted the staircase to the left. Waiting for him stood King Edward's servant bundled up against the storm that raged outside and threatened to breach the castle walls. The servant nodded to Dunham and motioned for him to follow. Slowly he climbed the narrow and chipped stone steps. At the top, a heavy wooden door stood ajar. The servant entered first.

"Sire, Mr. Dunham is here."

The servant stepped aside, and the man dressed in worn leather clothes partially hidden by his black cloak entered. His scarred hands reached up and threw off the hood, revealing a face weathered by life and by evil. A scar traveled across his left cheek from his prominent chin to the underneath of his left eye. So near to the eye, it caused the eyelid to convulse repeatedly. It added to the evil that flowed from the rest of his body.

As Dunham approached the king, the scent of saltwater enveloped the room. Saltwater and rot. The king dismissed the servant with a wave of his hand while at the same time trying to push the saltwater smell away. He didn't need to be reminded that he was no longer able to take to the sea to do his own raiding. His nose wrinkled up at the rotten odor of seaweed. It filled him with disgust that he was reduced to hiring an outlaw to do his bidding.

Dunham remained standing, eyeing the crippled man before him. He'd heard of the action that had left this king a cripple, but that didn't make him careless. The king was still dangerous. All Dunham wanted was an opportunity to earn a living by whatever means available. He watched as the king's eye spotted the brand on his left hand. The brand was plainly visible; he made no attempt to cover it.

"They said you carried the brand," the king said. "I wasn't sure if it was true."

"It is because of the brand that you find me here before you today." Dunham moved closer. "I need to earn a living, and what better way for a thief than the life of an outlaw?"

"You have no regrets about what you have done?"

"Only that now I must entrust my livelihood to others instead of myself." He paused. "But it has worked out. Nothing is a problem for long."

"Very well. Do you understand the task as it was explained in the letter?"

"Yes. You want the jewel known as the King's Ransom, and I can get it for you," Dunham said.

"That's right. And when you have it, you are to make your way to St. David's Head to signal the same boat captain who dropped you off here. It should take him about six days to reach there. He will wait two days for you to make contact. He will then meet you in Cardigan Bay the following evening and transport you across the Channel to France. There a buyer will be waiting for you. Upon receipt of the jewel, you will be paid and sent on your way. No further correspondence between us will be necessary unless I need your services again." The king stopped.

"I understand. And where exactly is this King's Ransom?" Dunham asked.

"It is at Pembroke Castle to the west across the peninsula. I've got a man in the castle who will take you to the jewel." The king paused, and Dunham felt the heat of his gaze over his face. "Once you have the jewel in your possessions, he is not to be left to tell the tale when you leave. Understand?"

Dunham defiantly returned the king's glare. Crippled or not, here was a man not to cross. "I understand. He will be taken care of discretely."

"And nothing is to lead back to here. Nothing, unless you have grown tired of your outlaw life."

"You will have no worries there," Dunham said. Then he turned and left the room.

The king allowed a grin to break out. "At last," he said to no one. "I will be able to obtain enough money to hire an army to attack Pembroke Castle and rid the peninsula of that insolent king and gain control of all the land east of the Western Cleddau River."

In the bailey courtyard Dunham was met by the servant leading a warhorse. He took one look at the horse and then shook his head. "I'll go on foot. Much easier to get the lay of the land. If I need a horse later, I'll take it from Pembroke Castle." With that he headed out of the castle gate and took a path to the west.

1

GAVIN

Gavin bounded down the keep steps, eager to discover the cause of the cacophony echoing through the tower. The snorting and whinnying of horses competed with the voices of knights calling to each other across the courtyard. He stuffed his green tunic into his black breeches as he ran. In too much of a hurry to comb his hair, Gavin tried to smooth the brown cowlick with his fingers.

As the youngest prince of Pembroke Castle, Gavin dutifully attended his daily lessons. As a page, he was learning to handle a sword in battle and take care of the weapons, equipment, and horses of the knights. Soon to be a squire, he worried about how he would act in battle. Well, not exactly in battle.

Squires tended the knights' horses and guarded the supplies while they fought. The unspoken rule of warfare stated that squires couldn't be put in danger.

However, others in the castle had talked about the times the enemy had sent warriors behind the fighting to attack the supply line. Squires who hadn't run away had been injured or killed.

Gavin worried about disgracing his family and the crown, worried that he would be scared enough to run or worse, get injured or killed.

The simple truth was, he was afraid.

Burying those thoughts, Gavin burst into the bailey courtyard amassed with horses and knights milling about. Dust swirled, choking the air, causing him to cough and sneeze. He recognized his older brother Robert across the chaotic courtyard and raised his hand in salute.

Robert led his black gelding over and handed Gavin the reins. "Hi, Gav." Robert tousled Gavin's hair.

"What's happening? Where are you going?"

"Someone broke into the throne room last night and stole the King's Ransom..."

Gavin gasped. The medallion was made of gold and embedded with emeralds so dark the jewels looked black except in the sunlight. Then the deep green sparkled lighter and reminded him of the first blades of grass pushing up through the dark earth in the spring. The tremendous weight of the medallion required him to use both hands when holding it.

Stories passed down said that a traitor over the channel

had used it to force a king to ransom his kingdom. To be in possession of it meant to be in possession of power. Many men wanted that power. Gavin's grandfather's grandfather had found it as a young man during the siege of a French castle. Though only seventeen, that prince had recognized its importance and had risked his life to bring it home. To protect his find, he'd spent the night in a storeroom listening to the screams of the defeated forces and the drunken laughter of the victors. He'd presented it to his father, and it had been in the possession of the King of Pembroke Castle ever since.

"...and killed one of our men," Robert finished, breaking into his thoughts.

"Who?"

"Aldred."

An image of the thin, wiry man appeared in Gavin's mind. It wasn't pleasant. Aldred had managed the estate and the castle's daily needs and also watched over the treasury. That meant that he frequented the throne room. Invariably he was with the king when Gavin needed to talk to his father. It bothered him that Aldred shared the private conversations he had with his father. It always made him feel unimportant. But his father would be upset at his death.

"As soon as Father and Sean get here, we're going hunting. Man-hunting."

"Might I go along as your squire?" Gavin asked.

Robert seemed to see the hesitation Gavin knew was etched on his face. "Not this time, Gav. You'll get your chance to join us soon enough. And Gavin..." Robert paused. His body stiffened as he spotted the king and his brother making his way through the crowd on his black stallion. "You'll do well." He mounted his horse and held out a hand. Gavin handed him the reins and watched as Robert joined their father, King Wallace, and Sean.

"You know your father's rule," a soft voice behind Gavin said.

Gavin glanced up at the tall, slender figure now standing beside him. Most days, Queen Katherine didn't look old enough to be his mother. But today, the sadness of Aldred's death had left its mark. He had learned that events that affected his father had the same effect on his mother. Her green eyes, which usually sparkled with laughter, held traces of tears. A frown replaced her usual bright smile as she watched her husband and two oldest sons prepare to leave.

Gavin was startled to see the grey streaks running through her brown hair. He hadn't noticed that she was getting older.

"You'll be twelve in a few days. Then you'll be made Robert's squire. It's tradition, and your father is firm on tradition. You must wait until then." She put her arm around Gavin and squeezed his shoulders.

Gavin nodded. Together they watched through the dust as the troop of knights, with the king at their head, rode through the gate, out across the moat, and into the forest.

As much as he longed to be with them, he couldn't forget his fears.

2

THE THIEF

Gavin wiped the sweat from his forehead, wincing when he grazed his sunburned skin. He tried to swallow, but succeeded only in pushing more dust down his parched throat. His arms and back ached from having wielded the iron sword for the last two hours. He longed to take a break.

"Prince Gavin! Pay attention."

"I'm sorry, Master." Focusing his attention away from his body, he faced his opponent once more.

The sparring dummy stood, waiting. With arms that stuck out from its sandbag body, it looked like the small boys the farmers hired to keep the birds from eating and damaging the crops. He had often watched them standing frozen in the fields, their arms outstretched, waiting for the unsuspecting culprits to land. Then they charged into action, arms waving and voices screeching.

"Now remember, close battle requires you to be faster and more accurate than your enemy. That is accomplished only with focus and practice." The Sword Master motioned for Gavin to start.

Frowning in concentration, Gavin set his stance. He spread his legs to shoulder width and lifted the iron sword above his head. The dummy waited for him, arms outstretched, reaching, and ready.

Taking two steps forward, Gavin let the sword fall straight down on the dummy's left side. The weight of the blow swung it around to the left. Gavin moved too slowly, and the turning target knocked him down to the packed ground of the sparring arena.

Pain rushed through his body like a raging river savagely pouring over its banks, spreading everywhere. Gavin knew his face betrayed the pain running through him. If he had been tossed about in a river, he couldn't have hurt worse. His body throbbed and his head pounded. When he looked up, the Sword Master stood waiting.

"Try it again. This time don't move in so close."

Gavin stood, brushed off the dust, and took his stance again, a few paces back. His eyes darted around the arena. *I don't understand why the Wild Man isn't here. He never misses my practices.* Puzzled, he drew his attention back to the drill, focusing on the target. This time when he struck the dummy, it barely caught his left shoulder. But with his body already battered, the blow still caused his face to scrunch in pain.

"Better. Again. Adjust back about half a pace. Remember, you want to be clear of your enemy's thrust, but near enough to be able to use your dagger."

Gavin took a minute to study his footprints in the dust. His eyes strayed once more to the edge of the yard. *Where could he be?* Shaking his head, he knelt to look closer at his prints. Then, sure of where he needed to stand, he took his spot and raised his sword for the blow.

"Stop!"

Gavin froze.

"Take your time. Don't hurry the downward motion. Take just a moment, and focus on where you are standing in relation to your enemy. If this is how close you need to be, you want to remember it."

Gavin nodded and faced the dummy. His shadow fell on the target before him. Closing his eyes, he sealed the position in his mind. Ready, he focused on the left shoulder and let the sword fall.

Without a break in his stride, Gavin brought the sword back to his side and then lunged forward. He drove his dagger into the neck of the sand dummy, imagining that he was saving the kingdom.

"This is what you deserve, you bloody traitor!"

"Fine job, Prince Gavin." The Sword Master pulled

Gavin back to arm's length. "Remember, once you plunge the knife in, pull it out to make the wound bleed. Be quick to avoid falling into your enemy's poisoned dagger."

"I'm getting better, right?"

"Yes. You need a little more practice in the correct way to fight with a sword, but you're doing a remarkable job." The Sword Master rested his scarred hands on Gavin's small shoulders. "Don't worry, young Prince. You will be ready when called to battle."

The Sword Master glanced around. "Where's your audience today? You know, the beggar who lives in the forest."

"He's not a beggar." Gavin ran a hand through his sweaty brown hair. "He's just lost for a while."

"And he told you that?"

Gavin nodded.

"Well, he didn't show up here today. Maybe he found himself." The Sword Master allowed a rare grin to soften his wrinkled face.

Gavin scowled. Not wanting to argue about the Wild Man, he walked to the water trough. He scooped a dipper of water and quenched his thirst, and then ducked his head and poured water over it to cool him and temper his doubts, at least for now. After tugging off his leather breastplate, Gavin started toward the weapons armory.

"Your Highness," the Sword Master called after him, "be sure Bryan practices with the dummy next time. The blacksmith's apprentice is doing better, but a few hard knocks won't hurt!"

"Yes, sir," Gavin replied, pleased that his sessions with Bryan drew praise.

Gavin grabbed a rag from the workbench in the armory and rubbed his armour to remove the dust. Next, he wiped down his sword, carefully checking for nicks in the blade that would weaken the weapon in battle. After putting away his armour and his sword, he climbed the smooth stone steps up to the south battlement. In peacetime, his father kept only a small group of knights on the outer wall. However, with the trespass into the castle and the murder of Aldred, a full company of knights now manned the battlements. Even the back wall, which sat high above the inlet, was guarded against an attack from the sea beyond. Dressed in battle armour, crossbows at the ready, they nodded when Gavin approached but returned to their surveillance of the surrounding land. Wanting to be alone, Gavin found a spot on the wall out of the way. With his feet hanging over the edge, he gazed down at the village and the land before him.

Despite the danger, the farmers were harvesting their crops. Once done, preparation of the fallow land for the winter wheat planting would begin. Below, husky oxen pulled plows in more than one field. Even the village children were hard at work, helping to pick carrots, onions, and turnips. All families gave the castle a portion of their crops to pay for the protection of the knights and to help feed them. The rest of the harvest was stored in earthen cellars next to the cottages.

Gavin's father was one of the few kings who never took money for what he considered his duty to the people. It hadn't always been like that. Before King Arthur came, outlaws roamed the land and preyed upon the common people. Families had flocked to their lords' castles, eager to pay whatever fees were demanded for protection. When the people couldn't pay, the king took their land.

King Arthur and his knights had put an end to the outlaws and the high fees charged the peasants and had made the land safe. Until today. Gavin couldn't even recall a crime in recent years under his father's rule. He'd never heard of a murder in the village or inside the castle walls.

A commotion from the gatehouse across the bailey courtyard reached him.

"They're coming! King Wallace and his knights are coming!"

"Do they have the murdering thief?"

"Yes! The knights have him surrounded and tied to a horse."

"Open the gates!"

King Wallace rode through the gate first on his black stallion, dust clouds following in his wake. In spite of the heat and the hunt, his father sat straighter and taller than the others, his black cloak lightly covered in dust. Gavin's older brothers flanked him, impressive, but still dwarfed by the king. They also wore the signature black cloaks with Pembroke's fighting stags sewn on the back. The knights followed, clad in their leather armour decorated with the fighting stags. In their center rode the thief, the murderer.

Gavin looked closely at the man trying to see what made this person so ruthless that he would take the life of another for gemstones. Many times his father had told him that some men needed more than themselves to make them feel powerful. As the king and knights dismounted, stable boys came to take the horses away. Two knights pulled the captured man from the saddle and he tumbled to the ground, shooting more dust into the air. Swords penned him down while the crowd moved in closer, their voices raised in outrage. King Wallace and his sons backed away from the prisoner. Then Gavin saw Robert hand something to his father.

The King jumped up onto a nearby wagon, and the crowd quieted as he held up his hand. "I bring justice to Pembroke once again. Before you is the killer of Aldred and the thief of the King's Ransom, a medallion long treasured by my father and coveted by others."

The crowd cheered.

Then he held up the blood-covered knife Robert had given him. "Behold, the murder weapon!"

More cheers rocked the castle.

King Wallace held up his other hand, silencing the

crowd. "This man will be held for King Arthur's arrival. His fate will be decided then."

The murmurs of the crowd grew unsettled.

"Either he will reveal the hiding place of the King's Ransom or be put to death at Arthur's feet."

The crowd cheered once more.

The King motioned for the guards to allow the prisoner to rise and be escorted to the dungeon. Then he and his sons left the bailey courtyard.

"King Arthur!" Gavin said in amazement. He never thought he would see King Arthur. Even his brothers had seen him only once. Gavin ran around the battlement until he was above the knights.

Eagerly he waited to see the thief and murderer for himself.

As the captive straightened, the shadow from the corner tower obscured Gavin's view of the man's face. The prisoner's light brown hair sent shivers down Gavin's spine. Moving closer to the edge of the parapet, Gavin gasped when the face came into view. "Bloody hell!"

As the captive was led to the guardhouse, he looked up and met Gavin's eyes.

"It is him!" Gavin fell back into the parapet, its cold stone forcing the breath back into his body.

Earlier

Dunham had watched from the trees as the king's men apprehended their suspect. He'd chuckled to himself, a wicked sound had anyone been listening, almost like the devil laughing. That would take care of any trail leading back to that old renegade king. His job nearly complete, he left and headed on his way.

3

PHILIP

The late afternoon sun still held the day's heat. Philip set the ax down and wiped his brow before getting a drink of water. Across the valley, the walls of Pembroke Castle rose. Its gates stood open, although they were heavily guarded. Come dusk, those gates would be closed, and more than the usual number of knights would be on the parapets. Rumors had spread of the murder and theft this morning.

Since then, the village had been on edge. Farmers didn't stray far from their fields and kept their children close to home. Additional knights patrolled Pembroke village and the surrounding lands.

Philip had watched the king and his knights ride out this morning. Gavin hadn't been among them. They had returned just a short while ago. If the shouts from the castle were any indication, the murderer had been caught. The villagers would rest easy tonight, but the guard wouldn't be dropped. Until it was known for sure that the culprit had acted on his own, King Wallace would keep extra knights on duty.

Philip had never spoken to the king, but he admired him. The people of Pembroke had not turned him away that cold winter day a year ago. Instead, they offered him shelter and protection. With the consent of the king, the friar gave him a home in the church. In return, Philip helped the friar in the fields and with other chores, grateful for a safe place to stay.

Looking at the stack of chopped wood, he smiled sadly. Two years ago he never would have dreamed he'd be here, chopping wood for food and a dry place to sleep. He shook his head at his thoughts, his shaggy, ill-cut black hair falling unevenly across his forehead. Two years. It seemed like forever.

Two years earlier, he had lived with his parents and baby brother on their small farm up north. His parents worked hard to put food on the table and to pay off the farm. Philip's main job was to watch baby Benjamin while his mother helped his father in their small field. When Benjamin fell sick, Philip helped his father clear the old stalks and rocks from the soil while his mother nursed the baby. He helped his father carefully plant the winter wheat and barley for harvest in the spring.

As autumn slipped into winter, Benjamin hadn't gotten better. His tiny body burned with fever. Those last few days when Philip held him, the heat coming from Benjamin threatened to slowly engulf him like the embers of a dying fire.

Then one day, the heat drained from Benjamin's body, and cold took its place. Philip didn't understand at first why his mother and father cried. For days they'd waited for the fever to leave, and finally it had. Then he noticed the stillness of Benjamin's body. His small chest didn't rise and fall; he wasn't breathing. Along with the heat, life had also left the tiny body.

They buried Benjamin under a layer of straw in the small ditch next to the cottage, dressed in his little clothes, his body wrapped tightly in a blanket. Philip wept openly beside his parents, not ashamed to show his grief. Unknown to him then, it was just the beginning.

Philip blinked as tears threatened to fall. After more than a year, pain still stabbed at his heart. He didn't think that hollow empty feeling would ever leave.

Taking a deep breath, he reached for another log to split. *Boys don't cry, no matter what.* He wiped dirt across his face, hiding his tears. His secret couldn't be discovered. Raising the ax, he brought it down again and again, hoping the sound would fill his head and push the memories away, but they came anyway.

Three weeks after the death of Benjamin, his father had come in from cutting wood. Sweat poured down his face even as the first winter storm pelted the land with snow and the wind raged. Philip, filled with fear, drew water from the well while his mother helped his father into bed.

"Philip, bring me another blanket."

Philip did as he was asked and watched his father try to fight the bedclothes.

"Bring me the washcloth and water."

Nervously, Philip did. They took turns bathing his father's face with the cool water. When he held his father's hand, the heat burned his skin just as Benjamin's had. It took just three days for the heat to burn his father's life away. Three days.

Philip helped his mother drag his father's body to the ditch where Benjamin lay. As with his brother, they covered his father with straw and stones. Numb with shock and cold, they stood, hanging onto each other, tears streaming down their faces.

Two days later, Philip came in with more wood for the stove and found his mother lying on the floor in front of the hearth. Philip rushed to her side and bent over her. He placed his hand on his mother's face, and then pulled it back, afraid. Her skin was on fire. Philip sat back on the packed dirt floor, as if frozen in time, unable to believe or understand. Then he got up and grabbed the water bucket and the washcloth. Tenderly he tried to cool his mother's skin, wiping gently, willing the cool water to work.

She had lasted only through the night. At morning's first light, her life was gone. Winter's cold settled deep in Philip's bones as he rolled his mother's body onto a blanket. Gently he pulled her outside and to the ditch where his father and baby brother rested. There he laid his mother on the other side of Benjamin and covered her with straw and stones.

He stood there most of the day, staring at the graves of his family, not knowing what to do. As dusk approached, he moved inside and sat. Numb. He waited. And waited. But nothing happened. All through the night, he stayed awake, checking his skin, waiting for the heat to start. He didn't move the next day or for two more days. He didn't eat. He didn't drink. He just waited to die, for the heat to consume his life so he could be with his family. But the heat of the fever hadn't come. He hadn't died.

Philip struggled against the hurt and the memories. He stared out past the abbey, knowing that if the Wild Man had shown up, he would have helped keep his memories at bay. His absence fueled those memories, allowed them to surface. Philip had become attached to the man's gentle voice, so like his father's, at once.

With the Wild Man, he forgot, even for a short time, the guilt that engulfed him, that threatened to drown him like the cold murky waters of the northern marshes. His father had told him of men who dared to tread through those marshes. If they missed a step, they plunged down into the darkness, no saving breath possible, just a brief struggle before life left their bodies.

Philip felt like that when the grief overtook him, unsure if he would or even if he wanted to survive the next minute, hour, or day.

He should have refused the Wild Man's help and his company when he'd arrived in Pembroke. It had been a relief, though, to find a friend and a place to call home, even if it would never be.

The Wild Man had introduced him to young Prince Gavin, as alone as he, but in a different way. Gavin feared disappointing his family, failing them by showing cowardice in battle. Philip had formed a bond with Gavin those first weeks that helped them deal with their fears and doubts.

In time, Gavin introduced him to Bryan, the blacksmith's apprentice. Bryan, sent away by his family to learn a trade, longed to be a knight, but he lacked the money and stature that would make it possible. And so Bryan dreamed of a life he would never have, could never have. He labored in sadness and silence.

Indeed, they all had their demons.

And Philip? While he had found a new family in his friends, he had chosen not to confide in them, yet. He was afraid of again losing those he had come to care about.

He dropped the ax and loaded the flat wagon with firewood, slamming each log into the bed of the wagon, shutting the doors in his mind, trying again to close off the painful memories. He took the reins of the grey donkey hitched to the wagon and pulled firmly until the donkey followed him to the south side of the abbey. There he unloaded and stacked the wood, stopping at times and gazing around, hoping to see the Wild Man. It was unlike him not to help with the wood.

A frantic voice interrupted his thoughts.

"Philip! Philip! Where are you?"

Squinting into the falling sun, he made out a small figure running across the field.

"Philip!"

"Hey, Gav." He raised his arm in acknowledgment of the young prince's shout.

"Ph...Philip," Gavin sputtered as he drew alongside him, his sides heaving.

Philip stood silent, waiting while Gavin caught his breath. "What's the matter? It's only an hour 'til we were to meet."

"You don't know? You...you haven't heard?"

The fear in Gavin's eyes made Philip gulp. "Heard what? About the murder and the theft? Everyone has heard about that." Philip turned back to finish stacking the last of the wood. "From the commotion at the castle a while back, I guess they caught the murderer."

"Yes, so they think."

Philip looked over his shoulder at Gavin. "What are you saying?"

"They brought back the Wild Man. Had him tied on his horse. They put him in the dungeon!"

Philip leaned against the wagon, stunned at the news. "What do you mean? How...why...don't they know they have the wrong man? The Wild Man couldn't, wouldn't kill anyone or steal anything! They are wrong!"

"They came back with a knife, covered in blood."

"No," Philip whispered.

"And King Arthur is coming here!"

"When?"

Gavin shook his head. "I don't know, but the Wild Man has until then to tell where he has hidden the jeweled medallion."

"And if he doesn't?"

"Then he will be put to death at Arthur's feet," Gavin said in little more than a whisper.

Philip slumped to the ground. Gavin sank beside him. "We have to help him," Philip said. "But what can we do?"

Gavin frowned. "The real murderer and thief must have planted the knife in the Wild Man's things. He must have known that another suspect would give him a clear getaway."

"But how do we find the truth?"

Gavin took a deep breath. "Let's find Bryan. See if he has any ideas."

"Does he even know they arrested the Wild Man?"

"I don't know. I came here first."

Philip stood. "Let's go."

Together they hurried across the field, anxious to get to Bryan.

4

BRYAN

The air inside the blacksmith shop lay dense and heavy, making it difficult to breathe for any who ventured inside. The fire from the forge still burned red hot, even though the bellows hadn't fanned the embers in some time. Fifteen-year- old Bryan submersed the newly formed sword into a cold bucket of water. Steam enveloped him, adding to the sweat already streaming down his face. With his free arm, he wiped his forehead and pushed back his soaked red hair.

The blacksmith, James, watched intently as Bryan Balyard lifted the sword out of the water, its blade cooler but still hot to the touch. Holding the sword in front of him, Bryan sighted down the blade's edge as he'd been taught. Straight and flat, just as it should be. He made a few short cuts to check its balance. It responded well to his moves. Bryan handed the sword to James for approval.

After checking its weight and doing a closer inspection of the craftsmanship, James nodded.

"You're getting better. This weapon is good enough for a knight of the Round Table."

Bryan beamed, his eyes reddened and watering from the smoke.

"I haven't an order from any of Arthur's knights, so make this your own."

Bryan's lower jaw dropped. "Mine?" he forced out.

"Yes. I know you practice with the older, heavier swords. A good blacksmith must know how the perfect weapon feels when wielded."

"Thank you, Master James."

"Don't thank me," James answered gruffly. "I don't approve of your desire to be a knight. Men should know where they belong..." James paused, "...and you are destined to be a worker of metal."

Bryan started to protest, but James continued.

"Bank down the fire. Make sure the metal is ready for tomorrow. Then go and try out your sword with young Prince Gavin and that Wild Man." James left Bryan to straighten the shop.

In the five years he'd been James's apprentice, Bryan had learned a lot. He made a sturdy sword, so James said. Two years still remained in his apprenticeship. Two long years.

Like most sons of tradesmen or farmers, his family had

secured this apprenticeship early on. At eleven, he and his father had made the three-day journey south to the Pembroke Castle blacksmith. At first, the prospect of being away from home, on his own, and learning a respectable trade, was exciting. More importantly, it allowed him to see and talk with real knights.

He spent every day learning how to forge stronger swords, tougher armour, how to shoe horses, and even make pots and pans. It was a satisfying trade and one that would ensure him a livelihood. But Bryan didn't want just a livelihood. Even now, only two years away from completing his apprenticeship, he still couldn't see himself working with metal for the rest of his life.

As long as he could remember, he had wanted only one thing: to be a knight like Sir Lancelot. Unfortunately, becoming a knight required not only training and equipment, but also the money to pay for all that.

A knight went through a long training period, starting at age seven as a page, moving up to a squire at age twelve, and then, if he was good enough, being given the opportunity to compete against others of the same age in the tests. If a squire passed those, then he still found himself in need of a sponsor to secure his appointment to the knighthood. And that took a king or a prince or another knight.

Bryan knew only one prince: Gavin. Nearly twelve, Gavin was ready to become a squire. As much as Bryan knew the prince would like to help him, he also knew Gavin couldn't. Even though he was a prince, Gavin also had to be a knight. And so, at fifteen, Bryan worked and sweated, sometimes even burning himself, to become a blacksmith, a molder of metal.

But his heart remained hopeful, and so he practiced sword combat with the young prince and the Wild Man every night, just in case. And now he had his own sword.

"Bryan. Are you still there?"

"Yes. Come in, Gavin," he called to the young prince as he scrambled around to finish cleaning.

Gavin and Philip entered the shop, gasping at the heat.

"Just about done," Bryan said. "I have to bank the fire for tomorrow."

"We need to talk to you. Something's happened," Gavin said.

"We'll wait outside," Philip said, "where we can breathe."

Curious, Bryan hurried to join them, forgetting his sword in his rush.

"What is it?"

"Let's go behind the shop. We need to talk privately." Gavin led them away from prying eyes and ears.

"Well?"

Philip looked at Gavin. "You saw it."

Gavin nodded and told Bryan about the murder and theft.

"James told me. He saw the king and his knights head out this morning."

"They caught the man late this afternoon."

"So quick? James figured the man was long gone."

Something in the eyes and manners of his friends told Bryan there was more. "What's going on?"

"They brought in the Wild Man, tied to his horse. I saw him when they arrived back at the castle," Gavin said.

Bryan's heart pounded. "What?"

"They think he killed Aldred and stole the King's Ransom," Philip added.

"Bu-Bu-But..."

"They had a knife with dried blood still on it. It looked like the one the Wild Man always carries," Gavin finished.

Bryan said nothing, stunned at the idea that the Wild Man could be a murderer and a thief. But what did he know about the Wild Man? What did any of them know about the Wild Man? He just showed up one day asking for work in exchange for a place to stay. James had turned him away, but not before directing the wanderer to the church.

"Do you think he could have done it?" Bryan whispered.

"What?" Gavin said.

"He's been here nearly two years."

"How could...?"

"What do we know about him before he came here? Nothing," Bryan said. "We need to think about the possibility, especially since Gavin said it looked like the Wild Man's knife."

Gavin started to speak and then stopped. Even Philip was silent.

"I'm sure he didn't do it," Gavin finally said.

"Me too," Philip echoed.

"I don't think he did either," Bryan said.

"Now we just have to figure out how to prove it," Philip said.

5

THE KNIGHT'S VOW

Bryan spoke first. "We need to check around. Someone's shifted the blame to the Wild Man. We have to find out who."

"Philip and I will find out what else my father knows," Gavin said, taking charge.

"I can check around the village in the morning. I'm supposed to deliver orders, so that will make it easy," Bryan added.

Gavin nodded. "Stop and see if Seanna knows anything."

Bryan swallowed. "The witch?"

"I don't think she's a witch," Philip said. "We had a woman like her where I come from. She was a healer, but people didn't trust her."

Bryan hesitated.

"People go to Seanna for herbs. Even my mother does," Gavin said. "But Seanna also has strange powers. I've

heard some knights talk of the things she knows."

Bryan let out a long breath. "All right. I'll see Seanna."

"Before we leave here, we need to swear an oath that no matter what happens, we will see the Wild Man proven innocent," said Gavin.

Both Philip and Bryan nodded.

"We can use the sword I just made," Bryan said. He left and returned with the new weapon, unscarred by battle, its blade shimmering in the early evening light. He held it out to Gavin, who grabbed it below the hilt and held it out for the other two.

Philip grasped it above Gavin, and then Bryan put his hand above theirs. They looked to Gavin.

Gavin cleared his throat and then in a voice deeper than normal, he recited the words he had heard so often before in the chapel, words that bound newly anointed knights to service.

"I pledge by the knight's sword–symbol of light in the darkness of evil..." He stopped and waited for Bryan and Philip to repeat after him.

"...that I will prove the innocence of the Wild Man." Gavin paused again, while the others repeated the oath.

Gavin nodded at them and placed his other hand atop the sword's hilt. Philip and Bryan did the same.

"Should any of us be unable to continue," Gavin said, waiting as Bryan and Philip solemnly repeated the words, "then the others will carry forth this quest," he paused, "until either the Wild Man is free or none of us remains alive. Failure is not acceptable." Gavin looked hard at each of them. He waited, giving them time to think about their pledge, waited for them to acknowledge their understanding. First Philip, and then Bryan, nodded.

"We freely take up this quest and vow to remain loyal to and courageous for the Wild Man," Gavin finished, and the others repeated after him.

One by one they released the sword. Gavin, being the last, held the sword out flat in both hands to Bryan.

"Bryan, Philip, and I entrust the safety of this knight's sword to you. Do you accept it?"

"I do," Bryan said without hesitation, grasping the sword by the hilt.

"Well, it's done," Gavin said. "We'll meet behind the mill tomorrow evening. I hope by then we'll have enough information to decide what we can do to help the Wild Man."

6

SPYING

With the routine of the castle broken by the murder of Aldred and the subsequent capture of his killer, Gavin and Philip moved cautiously the next morning.

Philip followed the prince into the keep. He endured the curious stares of people they passed, but no one tried to stop them.

Philip hadn't slept, and from Gavin's reddened eyes, he hadn't either. Philip thought he saw evidence of tears, although Gavin would never admit it. His own eyes probably looked the same, and he wouldn't admit it either. The possibility of the Wild Man being put to death worried them both.

As they approached the keep, Philip balked. "Are you sure?"

Gavin nodded. "I know my father and brothers will meet soon. This is the only way to find out what they know."

"But, if they catch us..."

"They won't. There's a hidden passage behind the throne room. I'm the only one who's used it for years. I've listened there many times."

"Listened—about what?"

"They talk about the battles they've been in and how to protect our people," Gavin said, glancing away. "I have to know what to expect in my first battle. I can't fail my father or our people."

Philip nodded. "Let's go."

Gavin led the way, moving through the spacious halls with ease. Philip was as equally uncomfortable inside the castle walls and tried to look like he belonged, but his gaze darted down each corridor they passed, afraid they might be stopped. They met only one young girl, plainly dressed, who glanced away as they passed. Everyone recognized Gavin throughout the castle.

Though he tried to keep track of the turns Gavin made, Philip became lost as they went down a set of stairs to the right and then took another staircase up and turned left. They seemed to be walking in circles.

Gavin stopped in front of a tapestry whose bright colors had long ago faded. Still visible, however, was the scene depicting a royal stag. Philip recognized the stag, its proud head held high, its regal stance, and its color...white.

Even he had heard of the white stag. The tales told

of kings whose hunts for the animal had destroyed their kingdoms. It was said only the one true king of all Britain would succeed in capturing the white stag. And, if the king released the stag, his kingdom would stand forever, his descendants ruling until none were left. There was talk among the villagers that King Arthur had done just that, and he was the true king of all Britain.

Gavin's hand on his arm pulled Philip back from his musings. Gavin raised a corner of the tapestry and disappeared behind it. Philip followed, trembling as he touched the cloth of legend.

Gavin waited in a cramped hallway so small they had to duck to keep their heads from hitting the boards overhead.

Gavin leaned close and whispered, "The throne room is just around that corner."

Philip's gaze followed his friend's outstretched arm.

"We have to be quiet from now on. Even a whisper will give us away."

Philip nodded. Silently he followed Gavin. Only slivers of light from between the wooden slats lit the dark passageway. As they rounded the corner, voices seeped through the walls.

"I don't know whether he did it or not. We'll keep the guard doubled until we know for certain."

"Father, he had to have done it. The bloody knife was found in his blanket," argued Sean. "We don't know where he's from or how he came to be here. Besides, how could he have gotten inside the castle if Aldred didn't know him?"

"I'm not so certain he killed Aldred," said Robert. "He's pretty harmless from what I've heard and seen."

"What do you mean 'harmless'?" Sean asked. "He killed Aldred to cover up the theft and to keep him from spreading the alarm."

"I've seen him with Gavin and his friends, Philip and Bryan."

"What?"

"The boys worship him. He often watches Gavin practice and gives him good suggestions for improvement. I've even seen him instructing Bryan in sword fighting. He's handy with a sword. He also works for the friar and helps Philip with repairs around the church."

"I don't call a stranger who shows up out of nowhere and is good with a sword 'harmless.' And why's a man like that passing time with a prince of Pembroke?" Sean asked.

"That has little bearing here," King Wallace pointed out.

"I disagree. The people are angry over Aldred's death. I'm afraid if we don't convict this Wild Man, the people may take that to mean we are unwilling to prosecute a guilty man because of his friendship with Gavin," Sean said. "Maybe that's what he counted on."

Philip gripped Gavin's arm. What if the Wild Man had killed Aldred and stolen the King's Ransom? What if he'd used Gavin's friendship to do just that? What if the Wild Man had used them all? Philip calmed himself and squeezed Gavin's arm harder, knowing he was thinking the same thing. When Gavin turned, Philip shook his head and mouthed the word "No!" twice.

Gavin nodded.

"The people do not enforce the law here. I do!" King Wallace declared. "I'll decide if the man is guilty or not, and the people will live with my decision."

"As you say, Father," both sons replied, subdued.

"It troubles me that there was no sign of the King's Ransom with this...this Wild Man's belongings," the King continued. A chair scraped on the floor. The noise made Philip jump. He relaxed when someone, probably the king, paced.

"Why keep the knife and not the medallion?" King Wallace asked. "You two take a small contingent of knights tomorrow and search his camp. Find that medallion. He must have hidden it nearby, knowing it would be worthless around here. Probably planned on leaving the area after the uproar calmed down, never thinking we would be able to follow his trail so quickly. I bet he has a buyer for it." The king pounded his desk with his fist.

Gavin and Philip jumped.

"That's it! And I'd wager his buyer is King Edward," the king said.

"Of Manorbier Castle?" Sean asked.

"Why not? You've heard him threaten often enough that he'd like nothing better than to buy up all of Pembroke and get rid of us for good."

"Why don't we confront him? That might throw him off guard," Robert suggested.

"No. Unless we have proof, King Arthur would have my head if I provoked a conflict. It took him long enough to convince Edward to end his raids. Confronting him isn't the answer."

The scraping of chairs startled Gavin and Philip again.

"Go out tomorrow. Search well. When you return, have the knights question the villagers. If you turn up nothing, we'll apply pressure to our prisoner."

Both sons started to protest.

"I know, you want to question him now. However, some time without contact will put him in a more agreeable mood. Might make him eager to tell us where he's hidden the King's Ransom."

"What about King Arthur?"

"He will be here in four to five days. Either I have the medallion to present to him, or I give him the man's head. Close the door behind you. I need to think."

"Yes, Father."

Gavin signaled Philip to return the way they had come. When they reached the tapestry, Philip let Gavin move ahead to make sure the way was clear.

Once outside, they sat on a shadowed bench across from the dungeon.

"If we can't prove the Wild Man's innocent, then your father, I mean the king, will have him killed," Philip said.

"I know."

Both boys sat quietly.

Finally Philip said, "Gavin?"

"Yes?"

"Do you think the Wild Man would use our friendship?" Philip's voice trembled.

Gavin didn't answer.

7

THE WITCH

It was late morning by the time Bryan finished delivering the pots, swords, knives, and farm tools. No one he'd talked to had seen any strangers in the village.

On his way back to the forge, he stopped by the baker's. The smell of freshly baked bread made his mouth water and drew him behind the thatched house to the ovens. He found the baker working dough in a worn wooden bowl. Though he was a small man, the baker's arms bulged with muscles earned from years of kneading. He acknowledged Bryan by covering the dough with a cloth.

"I'm just about to take loaves out of the oven. Want some hot bread for lunch, young Bryan?"

"Yes, sir," Bryan said. His stomach rumbled as the smell surrounded him.

"Fill those mugs with water." The baker motioned to the bucket on the lip of the well. Bryan filled the mugs

from the metal dipper hanging from the well's crossbar.

After covering the just-baked loaves, the baker divided a loaf in two and handed a portion to Bryan. He tore off a piece and shoved it into his mouth. The warm bread melted on his tongue like snow on a hot spring day, hinting at the summer months to come.

"There is nothing better than your bread straight from the oven."

The baker wiped his hands on his apron and smiled. They finished the loaf in silence, savoring its taste.

When the baker rose to check the covered dough, Bryan dug into his pockets for money.

"No need, Bryan. Just tell James I need three more large loaf pans like the ones he made last time." He punched the dough.

"I'll tell him, sir." Bryan paused. Figuring he had nothing to lose, he continued. "Have you seen anybody around lately who doesn't belong?"

"You know, a stranger did stop here. Bought some loaves of bread, he did."

"How long ago?"

"Hold on. What interest is it of yours?"

"He stopped by the forge. Wanted an old sword worked on. I fixed it, but he hasn't been back. I told James I'd ask around today."

"It was three, no, four days ago." The baker stopped to think. "Might have even been five days ago. I'm not sure."

"Any idea where he went?"

"Sure. From here he went straight to the tavern," the baker answered. He looked up from the pan he was flouring and scratched his head, a dusting of flour remaining there. "Never saw him come out, but I wasn't watching. If he stayed until dark, it would have been hard to see him. He wore a dark cloak and the hood shadowed his face."

"Thank you," Bryan said. He hurried to the tavern, hope swelling in him. Maybe, just maybe, he'd get the information they needed.

He pushed open the heavy wooden door. The darkness and smoke from the peat fires blinded him. Once his eyes adjusted to the dim light, Bryan walked to the bar. The tavern owner glanced up from cleaning the tin mugs.

"Don't need anything yet, Bryan. In a few weeks I'll need to replace a vat out back."

"I'll let James know." Bryan hesitated. Lying didn't come easy for him, but the Wild Man was worth it.

"Did a stranger come in here maybe four or five days ago?" The tavern owner stopped his cleaning and rubbed his chin. "He would have been wearing a black cloak."

"Seems to me I remember someone like that. What's this about? This have anything to do with the murder?" he asked.

Bryan wondered what he'd say if he told him it did. "No. He left an old sword to be worked on. Hasn't been back since. Just tryin' to find out if he's still around."

"He was here, four days ago, I think. Believe he sat there in the corner where ol' Walter is sitting."

Bryan looked in the direction the tavern owner was pointing. "Did he happen to mention where he was staying?"

"No, and I didn't ask. I don't meddle in others' affairs." The tavern owner went back to wiping the tin mugs.

"Has he been back since?"

"He was here afternoon before last. Never saw him again though. Now you run along. I've got work to do and customers to wait on." He turned his back to the bar, shutting off any further conversation.

"Thanks."

Back outside, Bryan stopped to ponder. "If he was last seen two days ago, he could be the murderer," he said, thinking out loud. "Someone else had to have seen him, but who?"

Gavin's words came back to him. "If you have time, you could stop in and see Seanna."

"Guess I'll see for myself if she's a witch." He walked across the road and down a well-worn path that led to a small cottage at the edge of the village. Thinking about the Wild Man, he didn't realize he had reached his destination.

"Wondered when you'd get here."

Bryan jumped, jolted out of his thoughts. Looking around, he spotted the speaker, and even though he hadn't seen her up close before, he knew she was Seanna.

She was a young woman, not as old as the village gossip said. Her short, ragged-cut, black hair did nothing for her features. He wondered what she would look like if she grew it out. She might even be pretty.

He caught himself. "I must be touched in the head," he muttered.

Seanna seemed to hear him. "Come in and let me see if that's true." She went into her shop, a thatched cottage just like others in the village, at least on the outside.

Bryan hesitated, but this was for the Wild Man. Besides, he was too old to believe in witches.

"If she's not a witch, how'd she know I was coming?" he mumbled.

Once inside the shop, he stared. High windows lit the interior like the light of a full moon. Sharp spices assailed his senses, making each breath feel like his first. His eyes took in the shapes of dead animals, dried branches and flowers, and jars of various sizes containing things he could only guess at.

"Come," she said. "Sit here." She motioned to a chair opposite hers at a small table.

Bryan sat down.

"Pray tell," Seanna prompted. "What have you been doing this day?"

He frowned, wondering at her meaning.

"I've watched you. You delivered James's orders, but

since then, you've been asking questions. Have you gotten the answers you seek?"

Bryan shook his head, his eyes silently asking how she knew.

"Now that you're here, ask me. Maybe you'll be surprised."

"All right," Bryan said, taking another deep breath. "I've been

asking about a stranger who came into the village four or five days ago. The baker and the tavern owner talked to him, but he hasn't been seen since the day before yesterday." He stopped.

"Go on."

"He may have been the one who murdered Aldred and stole the King's Ransom." He sat on the edge of his bench, waiting for Seanna to speak.

"I see," Seanna said. She looked at him through her black eyelashes. "And what makes you think that? Yesterday I saw them bring in the man who did those things."

"That man is a friend," he said. "I and others believe he is innocent."

"Of course, young Prince Gavin and the...boy who lives at the church. Philip, I believe."

"You already know?"

"But of course. Didn't others tell you I know many things?"

Bryan stared at the floor of the hut, not sure how to answer.

"Tell Prince Gavin the ghost is a friend."

"What?" Bryan jumped, his eyes meeting Seanna's.

"And Philip..." she paused, her gaze boring into Bryan's. "Tell him that the darkness within the night will hide him."

"What do you mean?"

"They will come to know."

"You make little sense."

"Only to those who don't think." Her stare silenced his protest. "You seek information. I give information, accurate information."

Bryan stood, sure this had been a waste of time.

Seanna also stood. "One more thing, Bryan... Beware the danger in the sea." At that she walked to the door, folded her thin arms, and waited for him to leave.

Shaking his head, Bryan left. He stopped outside and turned to look at her once more, but she had already disappeared back behind the closed door.

8

THE DECISION

The sun neared the western horizon, and in the shadows, the light dimmed. Gavin and Philip waited for Bryan by the mill.

"Look, there he is," Gavin said, waving his arm to get Bryan to hurry. Once Bryan reached them, they moved around behind the mill where no one would hear or see them.

Bryan turned to Gavin and Philip. "What did you two find out?"

Gavin started. "My father is sending Robert and Sean out tomorrow. He wants them to go over the area where they found the Wild Man again. The King's Ransom wasn't with the Wild Man. Father doesn't understand why it wasn't found and the bloody knife was."

"Because the Wild Man isn't the murderer," Bryan said.

"What'd you learn?" Philip asked.

"I spoke with the baker and the tavern owner. They both talked to a stranger in the village four or five days ago."

"Could they tell you anything about him?" Gavin asked.

"Only the tavern owner. He last saw him the day before yesterday."

"The day of the murder," Gavin whispered.

"That's right," Bryan said.

"And Seanna?" Philip asked.

"She knew who I was talking about. She saw the stranger in town also. She was waiting for me," he added. "I don't know how, but she knew I was coming." He looked at Gavin and Philip. "She also knew you."

"I know," Gavin said. "I used to go with Mother to get herbs from her."

"No, I mean you, Philip. She knew you," Bryan said. "And the way she talked about you made my skin crawl. There's something strange about her."

Philip didn't answer.

"What did she say?" Gavin asked.

"Words that made little sense, but she had information for each of us. Gavin, she said to tell you that the ghost is a friend."

"What does that mean?"

Bryan shrugged.

"Philip, she said to tell you to hide in the darkness of the night."

Philip frowned. "What does that bloody mean?"

Bryan rolled his eyes.

"What did she tell you?" Gavin asked.

"To beware the danger in the sea."

"What could she possibly be trying to tell us?" Gavin asked, not expecting an answer.

"Don't know," Bryan replied. "Now what?"

"My father suspects King Edward of Manorbier Castle may have had a hand in the murder and the theft."

"Is he going after King Edward?" Bryan asked.

"No. My brothers wanted to do that. Father said no. Without proof he can't confront King Edward, especially with King Arthur arriving here in a few days."

Bryan stiffened. "King Arthur is coming here?"

"Yes. And if the King's Ransom isn't found, the Wild Man will be executed and his head presented to King Arthur."

"Is this King's Ransom really that important?" Bryan questioned. "One man has already died, and the Wild Man may be next. All for a piece of jewelry. Why?"

"It's because of the power that men think it has." He saw the doubt on their faces. "Not magical power. Years ago, it was the cause of rebellion against a French king. My grandfather's grandfather found it in that king's castle and gave it to his father. It is a symbol of absolute power. My family has guarded it for years. My father says it symbolizes justice in the right hands, and tyranny in the hands of someone like King Edward."

"So what do we do now?" Philip asked.

"We have to find out if King Edward had Aldred killed," Gavin said. "I'll go to Manorbier Castle."

"No one can get into Manorbier Castle. It's too dangerous," Philip said. "And you can't just ask the king if he paid someone to steal the King's Ransom!"

"Philip's right," Bryan agreed. "If you get caught..."

"I won't," Gavin insisted. "We need someone in the enemy's camp. I'm familiar with the kinds of people who work in a castle. I'll be able to find out what we need to know."

"What if someone recognizes you?" Philip asked.

"I won't go as a prince. I'll go as a traveler. We have travelers stopping here all the time."

"But a boy on his own?" Bryan asked.

Gavin noticed the strange look on Philip's face, but Bryan didn't.

"I'll be all right," Gavin stated.

"When will you go?" Philip asked.

"I'll leave tomorrow before dawn."

"Won't you be missed?" Bryan asked. "You won't be back before dark."

Gavin shook his head. "Not tomorrow. The king still has a castle to run, my brothers will be out with the knights, and my mother will be busy with the funeral for Aldred."

The look of concern in his friends' faces forced him to

go on. "I'll be all right," he said, trying to reassure them. "We swore the Knight's Oath to save the Wild Man. We have no choice. I have no choice. This is my test to see if I can be a true prince of Pembroke." He paused and then added softly, "I have to do this."

"We know," Philip said.

"Be careful. Don't get caught tomorrow," Bryan warned.

They shook hands, and Gavin watched his friends go their separate ways. Once alone, doubt edged into his thoughts. The memories of his nightmares made him tremble. He shook off the fear and then stood and stared at the castle, afraid he might not see it again.

"I wonder if this is how a knight feels on the eve of battle?" he said. "You can do this, Gavin," he continued. "You are a Pembroke Prince, and the Wild Man's life hangs on your courage."

9

GAVIN'S QUEST

Early the next day, well before dawn, Gavin had set out for Manorbier Castle. Now as he emerged from the dark forest that surrounded Manorbier, he reined in his horse, letting his eyes adjust to the daylight. Across the valley, dwarfing all else, loomed Manorbier Castle, perched on a rocky crag. Its broken outline sent a sense of foreboding through Gavin. Just then, the scent of freshly baked bread reached him and his empty stomach grumbled.

Nothing else, however, about the castle was welcoming. Evidence of vicious and prolonged battles marked its wooden walls; scars from fires set in an attempt to burn a way into the bailey courtyard covered the right side. Ugly scars. Black soot almost reached the top of the battlements towering above the treetops. Charred timbers remained, neither repaired nor replaced.

At the top, Gavin knew, dried blood left by defenders and attackers alike covered the timbers. It was the same at Pembroke, his home. The difference between the two castles was that his father, Pembroke's king, had bade his knights wash the worst of the blood off and repair the charred timbers after the last attack four years ago.

Though only seven at the time, Gavin often relived the battle in his sleep. He and his mother had hurried to safety, down in the cold dark dungeon. The thick dungeon door slammed and his mother slid the wooden bars into place, locking them inside. Even with the knowledge that two knights guarded the corridor outside, Gavin could not block out the battle and the fact that someone wanted them dead. Even after four years, all he had to do was close his eyes, and the chaos and death of that night returned.

Men running through the coal black night. Screams of wounded warriors echoing off the walls as arrows and rocks rained down. Shouts from Pembroke's knights for more water to douse the flames. Walls of water swept down the castle sides, knocking the invaders aside. Deep in the dungeon, Gavin could still hear the cries of the men. Those same cries continued to visit his dreams years later.

Here guards patrolled the parapet atop the castle battlements. The knights, armed with long bows and in upper body armour, paused at intervals to scan the surrounding countryside. Gavin shivered in spite of the warmth of the late summer sun and backed his horse into the shadows of the forest for protection from the knights' gazes.

Outside the open gate, two burly armed guards stood, sunlight glinting off their spear tips and breastplates. Huge iron swords hung at their sides. Their crossed spears blocked passage into the castle. Gavin would have to pass them to gain entrance to the castle, and he had no choice but to use the main gate. The only other way in was to scale the cliff that protected the back wall.

Between Gavin and the castle walls, the fields and surrounding cottages looked deserted. Only a few herds of sheep and cattle grazed in the sparse fields. At home, most of the villagers had at least a small piece of farmland. Whole families worked the fields, making the land around the castle bustle with activity. Here the fields were deserted.

Even so, he didn't want to ride through the village. A faint trail wound to the right, around the outskirts of the forest to the side of the castle. Taking that route would keep him out of the guards' sight until he was nearly at the castle wall. It would also be hard for them to tell from which direction he had come.

Gavin's gaze was drawn back to the castle's battle-scarred walls and the heavily armed guards. The evil emanating from the structure surrounded and held him captive, like a lone deer surrounded by hungry wolves in the dead of winter, unable to move, its eyes glassy with fear, its limbs frozen by the hypnotic gleam of the wolves' yellow eyes. Even knowing its life was ending, the deer wouldn't break and run. So Gavin sat frozen in front of the castle.

The enormity of his quest enveloped Gavin and he sighed. Continuing on meant he might save the Wild Man, but he might put himself in danger as well. King Edward was his father's enemy and possibly responsible for Aldred's murder. If Gavin were caught, Edward wouldn't treat him kindly. The young prince summoned his courage and focused on the Wild Man. It had seemed so simple last night in the company of Bryan and Philip.

He had dressed with care in the predawn hour, not wanting to look in any manner like a prince. His old, worn clothes didn't quite fit. His unruly hair completed the disguise.

He rode one of the older stable horses. Not wanting to answer questions from the stable master, he'd waited until no one was around and then led the horse out a back gate. White streaks of sweat now covered its withers and hindquarters, a testament to the effort it took rider and horse to cover the forty miles in under five hours.

As if sensing it was the subject of Gavin's mind, the grey horse danced around, anxious to move.

"What you think, huh, fella?" Gavin asked the horse. "Think anyone will recognize a prince of Pembroke Castle?"

The grey shook its head to rid itself of the flies that buzzed around his ears.

"I don't think so either."

Determined in spite of his doubts, Gavin increased the pressure of his knees, and the grey moved forward.

Nearing the castle, he studied the parapets. He counted six guards on the front, and they had long bows. Either King Edward was constantly under attack from sieges or he anticipated trouble. Interesting that forty miles away his father's castle was also heavily guarded.

As Gavin approached the gate, the two Herculean guards crossed their spears to prevent his entry.

"What business have you here?" one of the guards asked.

"Was gonna water me horse in the village, but the smell of baked bread led me here. I ain't had nothin' to eat since last night," Gavin answered, hoping he sounded like a farmer's son.

"Where you coming from?"

Gavin pointed north. "Me pa's got a place up there." He paused. "I'm on me way to 'Kom to meet a supply boat."

"Never heard of no supply boat puttin' in at Skomer. You?" he asked the other guard.

"Nah."

"Me pa said the captain be a friend and promised to unload for him there. That way we no have to go to Lianelli to pick 'em up." He held his breath, hoping they would believe his story.

The guard on the left removed his spear. "Ah, let 'em in. He's just a kid. Ain't gonna do no harm."

Gavin swallowed his retort at the insult.

The other guard removed his spear and motioned Gavin through the gate. He passed two more guards inside the portcullis. He nodded, but received only scowls in return.

Gavin dismounted and led his horse to the water trough. He was surprised to find so few people in the yard. This didn't appear to be a place where people wanted to be, much like the village outside. When his horse finished drinking, Gavin walked him to the stable.

"Hello?" he called.

"Whataya want?" a gruff voice answered out of the dark. The owner moved into the shadowed light. As he wiped his hand on his hide apron, the old man looked startled to see a boy standing there. His weathered face softened a bit. "Whataya need, boy?"

Gavin winced at his use of boy. "I wanted a place to tie up me horse while I get some bread."

The old man squinted. "Put 'em in that empty stall. I ain't cleaned it yet."

"Thanks." Gavin led the grey to the stall, but didn't remove the saddle. Instead, he just took the bit out of the horse's mouth. The old man threw half a section of hay into the stall, and the grey started munching.

Gavin had to get the man to open up. "Things are quiet around here."

"That a fact or a question?"

"It seems quiet. Not many people around."

"And those that are, mind their own business." The old man glared at Gavin and turned to go back to his work.

Gavin walked out of the stable, disgusted with himself. "You did a great job," he grumbled.

"Got insulted twice and told to mind your own business in less than five minutes." He ran a hand through his brown hair. "If I'm going to help the Wild Man, I have to do a better job of getting the baker to talk."

He walked across the yard. Amid the barnyard and rotten food smells, Gavin's nose picked up the aroma of freshly baked bread. On the other side of the castle keep, he found the baker's ovens. Looking around and not seeing anyone, he grabbed a loaf still warm to the touch and tore off an end.

"Hey there! Whataya think you're doing?"

Gavin turned to face the biggest man he had ever seen. The baker easily stood six feet tall, and to Gavin it seemed as if he was at least four feet across.

"So-sorry," he stuttered. "I only wanted a bite to eat. I didn't see no one around."

The baker stood with his enormous hands on his wide hips and glared at Gavin.

"You ever think of callin' out?"

"Uh, no sir, un sorry, sir."

"Well, no harm done, I suppose. What's a young'un like you doing here? Where's your pa?"

"Me pa's back home." Gavin pointed to the north, at least what he thought might be north. He hoped that was the general direction he'd indicated to the guards earlier. "He sent me for supplies. He knows a captain who's agreed to stop in 'Kom and leave the supplies there. That saves us a trip to Lianelli."

"Ain't never heard of any captain willin' to do that." The baker looked suspiciously at Gavin. "You sure you're not here to steal from us and King Edward?"

Gavin shook his head vigorously.

"Well, I'm not so sure of that." He started to reach for Gavin's shoulder. "You need to come with me to see the king. He'll have those guards' heads for lettin' you in the gate."

Gavin ducked under the baker's arm and ran toward the side of the keep. With the baker in pursuit, he sped around the corner.

Then the baker called out.

"Yo, guards! Thief in the bailey! Rally 'round the keep!"

10

GHOST OF MANORBIER CASTLE

Gavin didn't wait to see or hear any more. He left the side of the keep and ran across the courtyard. Angry shouts followed him. He dived around the corner of the stable, scrambling to get away without being seen. As he ran, a hand shot out of a side window and grabbed him by the collar. Gavin nearly fell from the sudden stop.

"Now, where do you think you're agoin'?" the stableman asked.

Gavin twisted, trying to break the older man's grip.

"Let me go. I'm not hurtin' no one."

"Let you go, huh? Not until King Edward has a chat with you." The man pulled him up and back to the edge of the window. He heard the old man curse, and the pressure on his neck lessened.

Gavin pushed off the wall with his hand. The old man lost his grip. Gavin landed face first in the dirt.

"Help! The boy's over here!"

Gavin jumped to his feet and took off running, rounding the corner of the stable. Ahead was another, smaller building, an open door right in front. Not knowing where else to go, he dashed through the opening and into the dark. The foul smell almost did him in. Gagging, trying to hold his breath, his gaze swept the darkness.

"My swords! What could stink so bad?"

Seeing the stench's source, he clapped a hand over his mouth to keep from throwing up. On the other side, lit only by a slit in the roof, lay the decaying body of a man. Unable to hold back any longer, he threw up. Still spitting and gagging, he looked again through watering eyes at the man. Wisps of white hair stuck out of the skull. It was impossible to tell who he had been. Some flesh remained, but only enough to discern that the figure was indeed a man.

Shouts outside brought him out of his stupor. He looked around, but saw no way out other than the door he'd come through.

"What I wouldn't give to be back home," he said. "I could die here. No one will believe the thief is a prince of Pembroke!" His stomach still queasy, Gavin searched the darkness for a hiding place. He moved further toward the back of the room and then froze; his heart skipped several beats.

Two lights shone in a dark corner. A quiet voice spoke to him. "Here! Come here! I'll halp you."

A small figure stepped out of the darkened corner, his frail hand extended. Ragged white hair like that clinging to the corpse sat atop the apparition's head. Gavin backed away, but the ghost followed. "Who...what...who are you?" he croaked.

"Don't be 'fraid," the apparition said. The outstretched hand still reached out. "You must come quick. The smell will keep 'em at bay for a while, but soon enough they'll search in here for you." The ghost turned and beckoned him to follow.

Having no other choice, Gavin did as he was told, even though the way took him closer to the rotting corpse. Covering his mouth and nose with his hand, he ducked behind the body, anxious not to lose the apparition.

The ghost waited for him at the back of the structure, and then disappeared. Gavin gasped and hurried to where it had been.

He reached out, and from the dark, a small frail hand touched his. Gavin nearly fainted. The hand grabbed his and yanked him through a slit behind a moldy hanging tapestry.

Gavin, who moments ago was sure he was about to be captured, now found himself in a narrow passageway between the building and the castle's outer wall. Standing in front of him was the ghost. Seanna's words played back in his head. *The ghost is a friend.* Gavin looked closer. The ghost was really a boy, probably about his age, with stark white hair and a body so thin, Gavin could count his ribs. "Amazing," he said. "Seanna was right, at least so far."

The boy put a finger to his lips, and then turned around and followed the wall. Gavin hurried, not wanting to lose him. Shouts came from behind them, the search getting closer.

"Check that building," a man yelled.

"Not here!"

"Go back and watch the gate."

Gavin didn't know where the boy was leading him, but he had no chance of escape on his own. Up ahead, the boy stopped. Reaching him, Gavin put a hand on his shoulder. The boy turned and gave Gavin a ghostly smile, only a couple of teeth showing. Gavin opened his mouth to speak, but the boy stopped him. With a wave of his skinny arm, he beckoned Gavin to step beside him. He motioned to a hole in the outer wall barely big enough for a small child to squeeze through.

"You need to crawl out here," the boy whispered.

"But I need to go home, and my horse is in the stable." He paused and looked out the hole. "The afternoon is nearly gone."

"You're not agoin' nowhere for a bit. Not with 'em still looking for you." He motioned back the way they had come, his white head bobbing like a cork in water.

"I've made a bloody mess of things." Gavin swallowed hard. "What do I do after I go through the hole?"

"Head for the tree line over there." The boy pulled Gavin close so he could see. Gavin's gaze followed the boy's outstretched hand. To the right, the forest had not been thinned. It was only a short run to safety.

"If you stay close to the castle wall, no one'll see ya. Once in the trees, follow the path. It leads to a small pool where I take the horses for a bath. No one goes there but me. Wait for me there."

Gavin nodded.

"When they get tired of searchin', I'll take a couple o' horses, including yours, to the pool. The guards are used to me doin' that."

"Why?" Gavin asked.

The boy looked puzzled.

"Why help me? You're bound to get in trouble."

"Nah, ain't no one gonna do nothin' to me."

It was Gavin's turn to be puzzled.

"I knows all the secrets 'round 'ere. I knows all about everyone 'ere. And they knows I ain't 'fraid to use them secrets." His pale face beamed with confidence. "They leave me alone."

Gavin nodded, still unsure.

"Go now. I'll come soon as I can."

"Thank you." Gavin gave him what he hoped was a brave smile and, after a glance out the hole, wiggled through. He hugged the wall, inching his way along until the trees were a giant step away. He glanced at the top of the wall and, seeing no one, dashed the short distance into the forest.

Safely there, he sat on the ground, his breath coming in gasps. For a moment, he was tempted to put his head in his hands and cry. He had failed to get any information that could help the Wild Man. He'd only put himself and that ghost boy at risk. If caught, both of them would meet the same fate as that rotting corpse.

He took a deep breath. The boy had said he knew all the secrets. Maybe he would know about the stranger.

And maybe Gavin would learn something that could help the Wild Man after all.

The sun was close to setting when Gavin heard soft footfalls on the grassy trail. He peeked around the edge of the hill and saw the ghost boy riding his horse and leading two others. Gavin took a deep breath and sat, waiting.

The boy dismounted, handed over the reins, and led the other horses to the pool. He turned to Gavin as the animals plunged into the water.

"It's clear. You kin go. Be sure to stay in the trees 'til you are away from the castle. If you keep headin' to the west, you'll reach the road beyond the village. From there you can find your way." The boy moved beside Gavin's horse and held the stirrup for Gavin to mount. "They're eatin' and drinkin' now. The gate is locked, but there's still guards on the walls."

Gavin held out his hand. "My name's Gavin. What's yours?"

"Tom."

"Thanks, Tom. You sure you'll be okay?"

"Yep. Them don't dare bother me."

"Tom, you mentioned you know what's going on around here." Tom's white hair bobbed as he nodded.

"I came here looking for someone. Someone who has done something very bad." Gavin stopped, not sure of how much to say. But Tom had saved his life. He could trust him. "This person stole something from my father."

"Did he kill a man?"

Gavin started. "How did you know?"

"I seen 'im speak to King Edward. But of course they didn't see me." His pale blue eyes sparkled with pride. "'Is name is Dunham."

"What else do you know about him? A friend of mine has been accused of the theft and murder. It's important that I bring back information that can help me and my friends free him."

"He had help."

"What? Who?"

Tom shrugged his shoulders. "Didn't give no name,

just someone inside the castle is all he said."

Gavin thought of Aldred, dead. It would fit. Why leave the one person who could identify him alive?

"This man, Dunham, he also had a scar, here..." Tom's hand drew a line down his right cheek. "Made 'im look even more mean."

"Did he say where he was going after he killed the man?"

"He's goin' someplace called St. David's Head to signal the boat that brought 'im 'ere. The boat will pick 'im up at Car...Car... something like that Bay."

"Cardigan Bay?"

"That's it. Cardigan Bay."

"Did you hear when he was to signal and meet the ship?"

"I don't keep up with the days very well. Nary need to." Tom scratched his head. "Should be soon. I think the king said that it'd take a day or so after the signal for the boat to get to the Bay."

"Let's see then," Gavin started counting on his fingers. "If he stole the medallion four days ago, he had to stay around to see whether the knife he planted in the Wild Man's camp was found, and the Wild Man arrested. How long before the ship will be in position to see the signal?"

"I heard 'im say six days."

"Six days. How did he leave here? On horseback?"

"Nah, I heard 'em sayin' he would walk and take a horse

85

from the castle over that way." Tom pointed in the general direction of Pembroke Castle.

"So, one or two days to walk to Pembroke, four days more before the ship is in position, half a day, one at the most to reach the ship." Gavin smacked his head with his hand. "Today could be the sixth day. The ship might be in position tonight!" Gavin jumped up. "I've got to get home. We can't miss him."

He mounted the grey and, looking at Tom, thanked him again.

As he started to ride away, Tom grabbed his leg.

"Gavin, if the man stole from your father, is you a prince?"

Gavin hesitated. "Yes, I'm the youngest prince of Pembroke Castle. But you mustn't tell anyone I was here. Understand?"

Tom's pale blue eyes shone brightly. "I'll nary tell a soul, Prince Gavin. I promise."

Gavin reached down to grab Tom's hand and shake it. "I promise that when we turn the thief over to my father, I'll make sure you're rewarded."

"The only reward I be wantin' is outta this castle. Can you do that?"

"You bet I can. Watch out for yourself. And thanks again." With that he turned and rode away. As much as he wanted to let the grey have his head and gallop home, he held the horse to a walk until he came to the road Tom mentioned. Then he dug his heels into the grey's flanks and held on as the horse exploded down the road.

11

PHILIP'S QUEST

Philip and Bryan huddled on the north side of the mill, protected from the stiff wind blowing off the water. Grey clouds pushed by the wind kept hiding the sun.

"Storm coming," Bryan said.

Philip nodded, his gaze never leaving the road from the castle. He jumped and pointed. "There he is."

They waited for Gavin to reach them.

"We stayed until well after dark." Philip shivered from the wind.

"It was after midnight before I got back."

"What did you find out?" Bryan rubbed his arms in an attempt to keep warm.

"A lot. And it's just as we thought, except there's even more to the plan. First, the man's name is Dunham." Gavin proceeded to tell them what had happened during

his trip to Manorbier. When Gavin mentioned the ghost-like Tom, Philip started.

"You know," Gavin said, "he looked almost like a ghost. And he nearly turned me into one when he came out of the dark."

"Can he be trusted?" Bryan asked.

"I wouldn't be here if it weren't for him. They had me trapped inside the castle walls. He smuggled me out and even managed to bring me my horse. That's why I was so late getting back. He made me wait until it was safe."

"If the timetable Tom told you is right, then tonight is Dunham's opportunity to signal the ship," Bryan said.

"How are we going to stop him?" Philip asked.

"We can't stop him unless we're sure he's got the King's Ransom," Gavin answered. "He won't contact the ship without the King's Ransom."

A gust of wind blew around the mill, sprinkling them with rain and making them all shiver and hug the side of the building.

"It's going to be a miserable day and an even more miserable night," Philip said, his mind wandering. Seanna said the ghost was Gavin's friend, and he was. *Hide in the darkness of the night.* Those were the words she had for him.

"We've got to find out if he makes contact with the ship," Gavin said.

"And the only way to do that is for someone to hike up

St. David's Head tonight," Bryan added.

Philip turned toward the sea, letting the wind-blown rain bite his cheeks. He had been unable to help his family, unable to do anything to save them. All he could do was try to make them comfortable as they died. He closed his eyes, shutting out the tears threatening to fall. He knew he wasn't brave, not like Gavin and Bryan. The only reason he'd travelled this far was because he was left with no choice. He couldn't stay at his home, not when people knew he was alone. It wouldn't have been safe.

The last thing Philip wanted to do was hike up St. David's Head after dark and in a storm, but that's what he would do if it was the only way to free the Wild Man. He would hide in the darkness of the night.

Philip turned from the sea and took a deep breath. "I'll go."

Gavin and Bryan stared at him.

"It's a long way in weather like this," Gavin said.

"This storm's only going to get worse," Bryan added.

"If he contacts the ship tonight, and we don't know it, then he will have won, and the Wild Man will die." Philip studied Gavin. The prince had already played his part. Whether he had been afraid, Philip would never know. He wouldn't ask. Maybe there was still a part for Bryan and maybe not. But Philip was sure that this was his trial, the only way to redeem himself for the death of his family. If he could do this, could face this danger alone, it's possible he would be able to rid himself of some of the guilt he carried. Tears threatened again, but Philip held them off. He couldn't betray his weakness now, not here. He had to be strong for his family, for the Wild Man, for himself, just as his mother had been strong for him until her death.

12

ST. DAVID'S HEAD

Scared but determined to complete his task, Philip waited by the mill for Gavin. The midmorning rain fell so heavily at times that the castle in the distance appeared an illusion, there but not there. Just as the magician caused those watching him to question what they saw, so the rain obscured the castle, making a stranger doubt its existence.

"Hey."

He started, the driving rain having hidden Gavin's approach. "Hi."

Gavin held the reins of the bay as Philip tied his provisions to the back of the saddle. Neither spoke; everything had already been said. It was up to him now. Philip mounted the horse, and Gavin gripped his leg.

"Be careful tonight. Keep the Wild Man in your thoughts, and you'll be okay." Gavin extended his hand. Philip grabbed it as one would a last hope, and then tried to let go, but Gavin kept hold. "Watch the road carefully. The rain will make it dangerous, especially the closer you get to St. David's."

Philip nodded.

"You should get there before Dunham, but stay alert. It will be hard to tell if he's ahead of you." Gavin gave his hand a final squeeze.

Philip nudged the bay forward, conscious of Gavin's gaze following him and still feeling the strength of the younger boy's grip. Gavin's parting words renewed his wavering courage. The prince had been afraid, but had still faced the danger at Manorbier. Philip could also face danger. He kicked the bay and headed northwest into the drizzle.

The rain continued the rest of the day. In places where the hills and trees shielded him, Philip was spared the full fury of the storm. Out in the open, the wind threatened to sweep him from the saddle like an angry wave might sweep a fisherman from his boat. Stubbornly, he and the bay trudged on, ever closer to St. David's Head.

If not for the rain, the jagged cliffs surrounding the Head would have been a beacon. As it was, he followed the coast, aware of the danger of meeting Dunham. From time to time, Philip stopped, but in the raging storm it was impossible to hear anything. He could only hope he was in front of the murderer.

After skirting the village of Newgate, Philip turned

west toward St. David's Head. The storm made the trip longer than expected, and he had gotten lost a couple of times. Twice he had mistakenly turned back toward the coast. It was only by chance that he saw his horse's hoof prints in the tree-sheltered mud.

"Bloody storm," he swore. "I don't have time for this."

It was impossible to tell when the sun would reach the horizon, but Philip knew time was running out. If he missed the murderer, they would lose Dunham. The Wild Man would be a dead man. He urged his horse to an even faster pace, risky in the heavy wind and rain. Philip knew the dangers, but he trusted the bay to get him there safely.

Even with his head buried in the black mane for protection from the wind and rain, Philip noted when they started to climb St. David's Head. Lightning lit the front side of the cliffs. He guided his horse toward a small grove of trees illuminated by jagged light. There, somewhat protected from the storm, he tied the bay. He would climb on foot from there.

Scrambling up St. David's Head proved to be a challenge. Philip hit a muddy spot and slid down several yards, cursing. He moved faster, to make up time. His quicker movements caused him to lose his footing repeatedly. His frustration mounted with each backwards slide. He could hear nothing, let alone see if Dunham was on the mountain also. He only hoped the downpour was as unfriendly to Dunham as it was to him.

"I'll be lucky if I ever get to the top. I need another lightning strike," he muttered. He pushed himself upward. It took several more minutes and more backward progress before his wish for lightning was fulfilled. With the few seconds of illumination it provided, Philip spied a trail to the left leading to the top. He made his way over and was rewarded with firmer footing provided by the rocks imbedded in the dirt. He made it to the top in half the time it had taken him to get to the trail.

At the peak, the relentless wind nearly toppled him. But Philip had too much at stake to be defeated. He hauled himself into the full brunt of the storm. Out to sea, the whitecaps rose and fell like his chest. His breathing, like the waves, was choppy and erratic. He stepped back from the cliff's edge and looked around. A blast of white light flashed across the sky, revealing a small cave to the right. There was no sign of Dunham. For a moment, Philip gave into panic. Maybe the murderer had already been here, contacted the ship, and gone.

With a sharp crack, another lightning strike split open the black night. The back of Philip's neck tingled. The flash of light exposed a ship making its way toward land. Tossed about by the waves, the boat fought the violence of the storm, making scant but steady headway on the rough water. He wasn't too late. He hadn't missed Dunham.

Another violent burst of wind hit him and he shivered, as much from the storm as the evil that he expected to encounter. Turning his back to the sea, he fought his way to the cave and the shelter it offered him. He waited, rubbing his arms, gradually losing track of time. The wind threatened to freeze his wet clothes to his skin.

He couldn't remember a colder night, except the first one he'd spent alone after his family was gone. Tears trickled down his cheeks. The memories rushed in like a river finding a weak spot in an earthen dam, slowly at first, and then breaking through into a cascade of swirling muddy water. Three graves in a frozen ditch. Three graves covered with straw and rock. Only he was left, waiting to die.

He was alone here, but he didn't want to die here. Not here, not alone. Philip shook away the painful thoughts. He leaned against the rock, its hardness keeping him in the present, his eyes focused outside, his thoughts on the ship, Dunham, and the Wild Man.

Another white-hot bolt of lightning pierced the night. Philip eased into the blackness. The next strike revealed a man climbing the trail. He didn't need to see the jagged scar to know this was the murderer Dunham. The violence of the storm enhanced the evil emanating from the man's body. Philip jumped back into the small cave, not wanting the lightning to betray him. *Hide in the darkness of the night.* Seanna's words.

Philip could barely breathe as the man reached the ledge, bent over against the storm. After considerable trouble, the murderer managed to light a lantern. Dunham opened his coat to shield the lantern. The lamp's light glinted off shining jewels. The King's Ransom, there in a satchel attached to Dunham's belt. A cry escaped Philip's lips. The man whirled around, facing the ledge and the cave, glaring through the storm.

Philip crouched and pressed against the cold rough stone, afraid to breathe. The hard stone offered no comfort now. He wanted to disappear into its granite shell. "Hide in the darkness of the night," he repeated silently. He closed his eyes tight. Better to feel death than to watch it coming. In the darkness, he asked the Wild Man and his family for forgiveness for his failure.

He waited to die. He hoped it would be quick.

13

BRYAN'S QUEST

A knock came in the wee hours of the morning. Bryan opened the door and shivered in the brisk early morning air, even though the rain and wind had moved out to sea.

Philip stood there, his soaked clothes dripping like the rain that had fallen most of the night. Bryan guided him to a chair and wrapped a blanket around him.

"We gave up shortly after midnight," Bryan said.

"The weather made the trip longer than we planned," Philip said. "But I saw Dunham. He was on the ledge in front of me. I saw him signal the boat. He had the medallion. I saw that, too," Philip paused in his ramblings. "I made a sound when I saw the medallion. I thought he heard me. I was afraid, may my family and the Wild Man forgive me. I was afraid of death." An involuntary cry escaped Philip's lips. He hugged his body as if trying to stop the shaking.

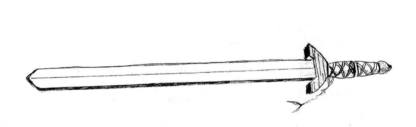

"I felt death. I closed my eyes and waited for Dunham to discover me and kill me. When I opened my eyes, a flash of lightning momentarily blinded me. But, Dunham was gone, and I was safe."

Bryan knelt and put an arm around Philip's shaking shoulders. Why was his friend so unnerved? Bryan glanced away, unsure how to comfort his friend. Gradually, Philip stopped crying.

"What do we do now?" Bryan asked.

"He'll meet the boat tonight. We have to stop him."

Bryan frowned. It would take time to rouse Gavin and explain everything Philip had seen. It would also take time to convince the King that the murderer was still out there. And one thing they didn't have was time.

Bryan ran a hand through his red hair. This was his opportunity to help the Wild Man and prove himself capable of being more than a metal smith. There would be hell to pay when he didn't show up for work. Even more when he returned, he suspected. But by then, maybe...

"I'll leave now for Cardigan Bay. The storm has blown out to sea, so I'll make good progress on the main roads. No need to skirt them now that we know where he's headed. I should get there before dark. That boat captain won't risk coming to shore any time before midnight. Too much chance of someone spotting him."

"But shouldn't we get Gavin first?"

Bryan shook his head. "No time. Someone needs

to be at Cardigan Bay to stop Dunham from boarding that boat."

"But..."

"You go to the castle and wake Gavin. Tell him everything you told me. Then you two convince the king to send his knights to Cardigan Bay. They should get there close to midnight if they ride hard." He held up a hand before Philip could say a word. "By then, I'll have scouted the place and have Dunham under watch. It will be easy for the knights to capture him."

Philip looked long at him. "Are you sure? What if he spots you?"

"I'll stay hidden. I'll be fine until the knights get there. You and Gavin make sure the king believes you. If the knights don't come, the Wild Man is dead."

"Be careful. He's a murderer. One more dead body won't make any difference to him."

Bryan grabbed his sword on his way out the door, not taking the time to reply.

He rode hard, not sparing his horse. It was in his hands now. His failure would mean the Wild Man would die along with his dream of becoming a knight.

After crossing the Western Cleddau River twice and using the main roads, he avoided the mayhem left by the storm, and rode into the quiet village of Fishguard early that evening. The fishermen were likely already asleep.

They would be up before dawn and the work of hauling in loaded nets was grueling. Only the tavern where he stopped to purchase cheese and bread showed any activity. On his way to Strumble Head, he ate and washed it down with the water he had grabbed.

He reached the Head at around eleven o'clock as the night was at its darkest. Only a sliver of moonlight forced its way through the clouds. It provided minimal light, but it was enough. He tied the grey in a stand of scrub well away from the trail, grabbed his sword, and walked to the point of the Head. The beach was deserted. His gaze swept the sea. Nothing.

"I'm here first. Now comes the hard part. Waiting." He picked a spot that afforded him good views of the trails leading onto the beach and the sea. There he sat, his right hand resting on the hilt of his sword, which lay beside him.

14

CARDIGAN BAY SHOWDOWN

As the night deepened, Bryan continued to watch. The moon weaved in and out of the clouds. At last, beyond the calmer water of the bay, he saw the ship, pitching violently on the waves, dangerously close to colliding with the rocks at the edge of Cardigan Bay. Bryan stood, sure that Dunham must be close.

There! Coming out of the brush halfway down the beach.

Bryan moved from his secluded hiding place, sword in hand. He hugged the shadows on his way to the beach, keeping an eye on Dunham. Once behind the man, Bryan paused.

The ship remained at anchor. In the moonlight, he made out a rowboat, rocked by the breakers as it was maneuvered over the rocks and into quieter waters.

Dunham splashed into the water, intent on meeting the rowboat farther out. Bryan looked around. No sign of Gavin or Philip or the knights. Dunham waded deeper into the sea. The rowboat made slow but steady progress toward its passenger.

If Dunham reached the safety of the rowboat, all was lost. The Wild Man, becoming a knight, all gone.

Seanna's warning raced through his head. *Beware the danger of the sea.*

Bryan ignored it, his decision made. With a warlike whoop, he raised the sword and ran for Dunham.

The man turned, startled. Seeing Bryan, he reached for some- thing on his belt.

In the dim light, Bryan caught the glint of something shiny. Thinking it was the medallion, he plowed headlong into Dunham, his sword braced to strike.

Dunham raised his left hand and blocked Bryan's sword, and then let the knife he'd pulled from his belt slice at his attacker.

As Bryan's body collided with Dunham's, he felt a sting and sharp pain in his left arm. His right hand loosened on the sword, but he didn't slow his forward movement. He continued driving with his legs, forcing Dunham off balance.

They hit the sandy bottom, the incoming waves washing over them with increased strength. The force of the impact knocked the sword out of Bryan's grip.

The cold water threatened to drown them both. Bryan groped for the sword. The salt stung his eyes and his injured arm. Still he refused to give up. Unable to find the sword, he wrapped his arms tightly around the man's body, unwilling to let Dunham escape.

Dunham went down again, coughing and spitting. As Bryan's arms tightened, Dunham twisted and wrenched out of his grasp, driving Bryan under the water.

Bryan gagged as salt water and sand filled his mouth and nose. His head pounded from the lack of air. Bryan fought his way up for air. His eyes watered, blurring his sight. He blinked hard and froze. The rowboat loomed closer, determined to pick up its passenger. Chills shook Bryan's body. No! He wouldn't be the one to let Dunham get away.

"Tonight is your last, whoever you are!" Dunham lunged at him through the seawater, the knife poised over his head.

"No!" Bryan yelled. He jumped to his right, into the force of the incoming waves. The waves' momentum pushed him back. Dunham, misjudging his position, missed. The knife sliced through air and water.

With an angry curse, he lunged again at Bryan, the knife poised to kill this time. Only one of them would survive.

The force of Dunham's attack drove Bryan to the sandy bottom, right on top of his sword. He felt the rough hand of his attacker at his throat. Holding his breath, he tried frantically to loosen Dunham's fingers with one hand while pulling the sword from under him.

The waves receded. He gasped for breath. Dunham squeezed harder. Bryan's vision narrowed. Both hands now wrestled with the hands around his neck, the sword forgotten as he fought certain death. His body grew weaker, the end near. Still Bryan struggled. For the Wild Man. For the quest. For Gavin and Philip. For himself.

Dunham's hands yanked Bryan's entire body, wrenching his neck. They released the stranglehold. Bryan gasped for breath as he surfaced, spitting out salt water and sand. Swaying, he fought to regain his balance. Hands helped him remain on his feet. As his eyes cleared, he looked around. Gavin stood on his left, Philip on his right, both supporting him. Bryan tried a weak smile, but ended up choking.

Strong hands gripped his arms. Knights took the place of his friends at his sides. He leaned on them and caught his breath. On the beach, King Wallace stood with Gavin's brothers. Behind him, Dunham struggled against two knights who held his arms. Another knight brandished his sword in front of Dunham's face, forcing him to quit fighting.

Beyond them, the rowboat hurried away, the men

pumping the oars frantically to return to the safety of their ship.

Bryan spied the wavering outline of his sword near Dunham's feet. He shrugged off the knights' hands, reached into the sea and pulled out his sword, his hand firmly on the hilt.

Bryan raised the tip to Dunham's throat.

The murderer's eyes widened with fear. Aware of the knights' stiffening stances and with a skill honed under the Wild Man's guidance, Bryan deftly cut through the satchel cord that hung around Dunham's neck. The King's Ransom fell into his hand.

Once on firm ground, Bryan faced Gavin and Philip, not wanting to appear afraid.

"You're bleeding!" Gavin said.

"I'm all right. A small cut, that's all."

"We thought you were drowned," Philip said.

"For a few minutes there, I thought so, too. Nice of you to take so long to get here." Bryan grinned to show he wasn't serious.

"It took a bit longer than I thought to convince my father we weren't crazy," Gavin said.

"I'll say it did," Prince Robert said. Reaching for Bryan's arm, he gently wrapped a rag around the area that was bleeding. "You took quite a chance facing Dunham alone. You might have been killed if we'd been any later getting here."

"I know. But if he'd gotten away, then the Wild Man would have hanged." He didn't add that he would have died also, still a metal smith.

"True, but you all showed a lot of courage. And you saved an innocent man." Prince Robert paused. "I'm not sure that I would have done the same."

"I think based on our actions and conclusions, we wouldn't have done what these young men have done," King Wallace interrupted.

The boys dropped to one knee.

"Prince Gavin. Bryan. Philip," the King said. "You have done this kingdom a great service. My eternal gratitude to all of you. Once we return to the castle, I will make sure that your service is acknowledged. And I dare say King Arthur will add his own congratulations upon his arrival tomorrow."

Bryan held out the satchel, his hand unsteady.

King Wallace removed the King's Ransom. The jewels sparkled in the moonlight. "Let's head home and put this murderer and thief in the dungeon."

"And free the Wild Man!" Gavin, Philip, and Bryan all spoke at once.

"And free the Wild Man," King Wallace echoed.

15

QUEST COMPLETED

On the ride to the castle, the three boys traded tales. Bryan shared his journey to Cardigan Bay and his confrontation with Dunham. He explained that he couldn't wait for the knights when Dunham waded into the water to meet the rowboat. Gavin and Philip took turns relating how they'd convinced King Wallace to gather his knights and ride for Cardigan Bay.

"He was skeptical," Gavin said. "Then Philip and I told him about our quests."

"When Gavin told him what Tom said, he believed us," Philip added.

"But when Philip described the jeweled medallion Dunham had stashed in his belt, my father ordered Sean and Robert to call the knights to arms," Gavin said.

"By then, the morning was half over," Philip continued. "We were afraid we might be too late. We almost were."

"We rode hard."

"If you hadn't, I would be dead, Dunham would be gone, and the Wild Man would have been hanged."

"It's still hard to believe," Philip said.

"Yes, it is. I'm shocked at Aldred's involvement. Father chose him as his advisor years ago. He's always trusted him."

"I'm sure Aldred expected to be paid handsomely for his betrayal of your father," Bryan said.

"He got lucky," Gavin said. "Father would have made an example of him and not a pleasant one."

"Dunham thought he'd found the perfect victim when he spotted the Wild Man and followed him to his camp. Planting the knife had been easy after that," Philip said.

"It didn't help that my brothers never trusted the Wild Man."

"But it turned out for the good," Philip said. "We saved him."

"Yes, we fulfilled the knight's oath," Gavin added.

"That we did." Bryan sat up taller in his saddle, proud of what he and the others had done.

The three fell into a thoughtful silence.

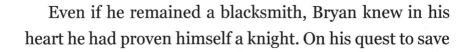

Even if he remained a blacksmith, Bryan knew in his heart he had proven himself a knight. On his quest to save the Wild Man, he had learned a man was only as good as his beliefs. His belief in the Wild Man and Gavin and Philip enabled him to fulfill his part of the quest.

Now he would become the best blacksmith he could. He would give his all, just as he had done in his quest to stop Dunham. That was what really made a man a knight. Loyalty and commitment to a man and a cause. He could show James loyalty and the trade his commitment. It might not be his dream, but he would always have these last few days and the friendship of Gavin, Philip, and the Wild Man.

Gavin's gaze swept over the knights. He imagined himself riding at their head, knowing now that he would be worthy to lead them. Together they would insure that the peace his father and brothers had fought so hard for was maintained. And if ever needed, Gavin knew that he would not hesitate to ride into battle. His determination not to let the Wild Man down drove him to face those nightmares that had haunted him for so long. He had been afraid in Manorbier Castle, but overcame his fear to fulfill his quest and gather the information needed to help the Wild Man.

When faced with discovery, he hadn't surrendered like the coward of his nightmares. Instead, he took steps to ensure he wouldn't be caught, and in the process, found the one person who could help him: Tom. And now, he would ask his father to rescue Tom from King Edward. Have Tom brought to Pembroke where he wouldn't have to worry about ending up like the corpse in the shed.

In time, he would rule the lands of Pembroke Castle: the forests where his father and brothers hunted deer, the marsh plains where the falcons and crows hunted, and the fields where the grains and crops that fed Pembroke's people were planted, grown, and harvested.

Gavin looked to either side at his friends. Their quest had changed each of them; Gavin could sense that. Now they were closer than friends, and Gavin knew they would only grow closer as the years passed. With Bryan and Philip standing beside him, he would grow into a stronger prince, no longer afraid to face his fears.

———◆———

Philip rode on in silence, still troubled. He hadn't mentioned his earlier conversation with the queen. While Gavin was helping with the horses, a servant had led him into the castle kitchen. There he found fresh bread and fruit waiting, along with the queen. As he bowed before her, she put her hand under his chin and tilted his chin until his eyes met hers.

"I have watched you since you first arrived, Philip.

The way you and Gavin enjoy each other's company, the sorrow you try so hard to suppress. Thank you for being a good friend to my youngest son. Gavin needed you. The other boys in the castle and the village have never been at ease around him. They see him as a prince and not a companion. His brothers are close enough in age to have had each other."

Philip nodded, not sure what the queen was trying to say.

"Philip, I have watched my sons grow, but my only daughter was taken from me when she was but two." The queen paused, her eyes seeming to pierce Philip's soul. "I always dreamed of raising a princess, one whom the King and I could love and cherish. One who would cherish her role and her responsibilities to the people of Pembroke."

Philip panicked. He tried to turn away, but the queen put her hands on his shoulders and held him there.

"I've watched you at church and with Gavin. You try, but you're no boy, Philip. What is your real name?"

Philippa blinked back tears. If this was the end of her charade, she would face the outcome with the same courage she'd shown on the mountain. She would make her mother and father proud of her.

"It's Philippa," she said, her head high and tears at bay.

"I thought as much. Gavin told me about your family," the queen said softly. "Is that the reason for this masquerade?"

"Yes. I didn't know what else to do," Philippa said. "I was afraid to travel the roads as a girl, but I couldn't stay at my home. It would have meant becoming a slave to anyone who found me. As a boy, I was free to travel and find work. Free to find somewhere to call home again."

"And have you?"

"I thought to stay here," she answered. "My father's clothes are so baggy that no one, except you, will know," she added.

"And what about you, Philippa?"

Philippa looked at her, perplexed.

"Do you not dream of having your own family? Your own children who will fill that empty hole in your heart?"

Philippa nodded, unable to speak for fear of the tears coming again.

"I have spoken with my husband, the king. Yes, he knows your secret," the queen said in response to Philippa's questioning look. "Long has this family dwelled on the little one who will never grace this castle. Gavin wasn't yet born, but his brothers remember Elisabeth." The queen hesitated, as if unsure what to say.

Philippa wondered what to do now that her secret was known.

"What I'm trying to say, Philippa, and failing miserably at, is that the king and I would like you to come and live here in the castle as our daughter."

Philippa's world tipped on its axis. She tried to speak

but the words stuck in her throat.

"We would take you into our family through the church rites. No one could challenge your rightful position as Princess of Pembroke Castle." She looked Philippa in the eye. "Will you consent to become our daughter? I realize you don't know us well or we you, but that will come in time."

Philippa wavered, her mind tumbling out of control like a pebble rolling down a steep slope. She didn't know what to say. What would Gavin and Bryan say when they found out?

She had been so lonely, in spite of having good friends. She needed to accept the queen's offer and to be herself. To look in a mirror and see a girl with clean hair, her clothes made for her, not for a man. A normal life once more.

"Philip! Philip! Wake up before you fall off your horse and get left behind!" The boys' laughter startled her out of her thoughts. She looked quickly around, surprised to see familiar surroundings. They weren't far from Pembroke.

"Sorry. I guess I'm a little sleepy," she replied.

Horns sounded as the turrets of Pembroke Castle appeared through the sun's last rays.

"Imagine how surprised the Wild Man will be," Gavin said.

"Will they release him right away?" Philippa asked.

"They should. Father knows Dunham is the murderer."

A shout from Bryan interrupted Gavin. "Look!"

Gavin and Philippa stood up in their stirrups, and smiles lit their faces.

Ahead, lining the road into the village and up to the castle, stood people, many people. The shouts and cheers started low and distant, but increased as the party drew closer.

"Father must have sent someone ahead," Gavin said.

"Look at the castle," Bryan said, pointing, "the flags!"

The flag embellished with Pembroke's fighting stags fluttered in the early evening breeze, but it wasn't alone. Above and to the right flew another flag. This one sported a pair of fighting dragons. Suddenly the knights cried out as one.

"King Arthur! Hail, Arthur!"

16

A SECRET UNVEILED

Once they'd ridden through the cheering crowd and into the bailey courtyard, the castle gates were closed, softening the cheers. Knights hauled the prisoner off his horse and to the dungeon. Gavin, Bryan, and Philippa followed, eager to see the Wild Man's reaction, but King Wallace stopped them.

"Gavin, you need to go with Sean and Robert. Your mother is waiting. You know the routine. As soon as her sons have returned from a quest, the queen insists on seeing for herself that all are well."

"Yes, Sire," Gavin said, a smile spreading across his face when his father put him into the same category as his brothers.

"Philip and Bryan," the King continued, "you'll find the friar and James waiting just inside the keep."

With the young ones out of harm, King Wallace went

to meet with King Arthur while the knights washed for a well-earned meal. Stable boys took the horses.

Shortly thereafter, Gavin watched from a window in the keep as his father and King Arthur left the castle with Arthur's contingent of knights close behind. He heard them return in the early hours of the next morning, but rolled over and went back to sleep.

That evening at the celebration banquet, the great hall was packed with knights and villagers. The fighting stags of Pembroke Castle adorned tapestries on the walls and the standards at one end of the head table. In the middle sat King Wallace, Queen Katherine, Robert, and Sean. King Arthur sat at the far end, his fighting dragons on the standard behind him, and an empty seat next to him. Hanging from a leather scabbard over the back of Arthur's chair was the fabled sword Excalibur. Gavin and Bryan sat at the left end of the table, an empty spot for Philip between them.

Gavin joined Bryan and the others in cheers when the servants entered carrying platters piled high with roasted pig, duck, and pheasant. Bowls of boiled carrots and onions and trays of freshly baked bread were set before him causing his stomach to growl. Gavin chuckled as raucous laughter died down and guests enjoyed the feast.

"Any idea where Philip is?" Bryan asked as they ate.

"No," Gavin replied. "And where is the Wild Man?"

They looked at the empty seat next to King Arthur.

"Your father, I mean, the king, released him, didn't he?"

"Late last night. Robert and Sean saw to it, my mother said."

"This is strange. No Philip and no Wild Man." Bryan shook his head.

When the noise in the hall signaled the end of the eating, Gavin noticed that his mother's seat was also empty. He wasn't sure what was going on, but it didn't seem right. Two people who deserved to be here were missing.

King Wallace stood and pounded his cup on the table to get the crowd's attention.

"Thank you all for being here," he began. "Tonight is special for all of us. We are gathered to honor not just a member of the royal family." He paused, and Gavin's face grew warm as the hall's attention centered on him. "But to honor two others." He paused again before continuing. "The queen and I also have an announcement to make."

Gavin and Bryan stood with the crowd as the queen entered the hall from the rear with Philip—except Philip was a girl!

Philippa's simple ankle-length gown of deep burgundy brought girlish life to her slim boyish body. Her once roughly cut brown hair, now clean and freshly trimmed, framed her face. Her chin quivered visibly, and her right hand clutched the queen's in a death grip.

Gavin was the first to find his voice. "Philip's wearing a dress!"

Bryan could only stare. The boy he had consoled just forty-eight hours ago was walking down the aisle with the queen. "What the bloody...?"

King Wallace's hearty laugh rang out as he looked from Gavin and Bryan to the guests. He bowed as his wife approached him and smiled when she stepped aside and handed Philippa's hand into his. Gently he kissed it, and then turned Philippa to face the people.

"Honored Guests, King Arthur and his knights, Bryan Balyard, my sons, Princes Robert, Sean, and Gavin, my loyal knights, and the people of Pembroke. Queen Katherine and I would like to introduce you to the newest member of the royal family." At that, he put his arm around Philippa's shoulders as the queen took her left hand and raised it in the air. "We are proud to present Princess Philippa, our daughter!"

A complete hush fell over the crowd. Gavin and Bryan fell into their seats.

Before Philippa's tears could start, King Arthur held up his goblet.

"To Princess Philippa. May her brave and unselfish deed long be the inspiration for other young maidens. May it be sung through time. May she continue to bring good fortune to Pembroke, and may she come to think of all you good people as her family."

Sean and Robert raised their goblets to signal their approval. The friar and James, seated below, held their goblets high. "Hear, hear!" they shouted.

At that the hall broke out in hearty cheers, with all goblets raised. Gavin and Bryan raised their goblets, too, wide grins across their faces.

Tears ran down Philippa's face, tears of joy she was unable to stop. Her dream of a family had come true.

She had spoken with the queen about her mother, father, and little brother, how she was afraid she might be betraying them. Both the queen and the friar had assured her that Philippa's family would have wanted her to be loved and cared for.

Now, as she took her place between Gavin and Bryan, their sincere smiles and hardy handshakes convinced her she had done the right thing.

"Boy, Philip, Philippa," Gavin said. "My best friend is my sister. Now we'll never be apart!"

"Uh, Philippa," Bryan stuttered. "I'm glad to see that you're a girl. I mean, that you're not a boy, uh, you know what I mean," he finished. Gavin and Philippa laughed.

"It's strange, I know," Philippa said, suddenly shy with Bryan's eyes on her.

"You could have told us," Bryan said. "We would have kept your secret."

"I, uh..."

"No he—she couldn't." Gavin giggled. "Then we

wouldn't have had this great surprise!"

Bryan and Philippa joined in his laughter.

King Wallace banged his goblet on the table in a call for silence and the three took their seats. All looked expectantly at him. But before King Wallace could continue, a commotion arose at the rear door of the hall. Several knights entered, pushing a man ahead of them.

"It looks as though our final guest has arrived, although it took considerable convincing from my knights." The crowd guffawed, and the man bowed his head, plainly embarrassed.

"Look!" Gavin pointed. "It's the Wild Man."

"He looks so different," Philippa exclaimed. "His clothes, his hair."

"He doesn't look happy to be here," Bryan noted.

The Wild Man was barely recognizable. His clean clothes fit and his brown hair had been trimmed and combed. But the look on his face left no doubt that this was the last place he wanted to be. The knights behind him kept moving him forward until they all stood in front of the head table.

"Maybe he was embarrassed to come," Bryan whispered. "I'm sure he didn't want to be laughed at."

Unnoticed, King Arthur stood.

The Wild Man raised his eyes to King Wallace, and then his gaze strayed to King Arthur. The two men studied each other, not breaking eye contact. Arthur's left eyebrow arched. The Wild Man let a slight smile show, and then turned his attention to King Wallace.

17

ANOTHER SECRET REVEALED

"King Arthur, knights, gentlemen, and ladies. I present to you for the first time in days, the free man known as the Wild Man and his three avengers, Prince Gavin, Princess Philippa, and Bryan Balyard."

Gavin stood with his friends, and waited as the Wild Man walked to the table. The Wild Man shook Gavin and Bryan's hands, but bowed to Philippa and touched his lips to her hand. He whispered something to her, but Gavin couldn't hear amid the cheers of the crowd and the banging of cups on the tables. He noticed the confused look on her face and wondered what had been said.

While the Wild Man took his place at the table, Gavin's father held up his hand to quiet the hall.

"Before we reward these young people, I would like to present King Arthur with a token of our friendship, and our loyalty to his cause of a united England."

Gavin covered his ears when the crowd responded even more exuberantly, obviously enjoying the free mead and ale.

"King Arthur," King Wallace's voice boomed, and Gavin flinched. "It is our honor to present you with the King's Ransom, as a symbol of the loyalty of everyone under my rule." He held out the medallion to King Arthur, but the king refused to take it.

"I think that it is only right, King Wallace, that I receive this from the hands of someone for whom it means life itself."

"As you wish," King Wallace murmured. "And who would that be, Your Majesty?"

"I believe it would be more appropriate for Sir Lancelot to present it to me."

Murmurs ran through the hall. No one remembered seeing the famous knight in the hall. Still, King Arthur stood, waiting for the knight to come forward. The Wild Man stood and all eyes focused on him. Gavin found himself unable to utter a word. When Bryan and Philippa looked at him, Gavin could only shrug his shoulders.

The silence in the room was deafening as the Wild Man walked to King Wallace and accepted the medallion and returned to Arthur's side.

Dropping to one knee, Sir Lancelot held the King's Ransom raised in both his hands for Arthur to take.

"Your Majesty," Sir Lancelot said. "I humbly present you with the King's Ransom and pledge my life and the return of my service to you and Queen Guinevere."

Gavin covered his mouth with his hand. He was vaguely aware of Bryan falling into his seat. "A knight!" He and his friends had saved a knight, and not just any knight. Sir Lancelot! Gavin grabbed Bryan's hand and pulled him up.

Bryan turned and pounded Philippa on the back, and then stopped, embarrassed when Gavin winked at him. "Sorry. Did you hear that? A knight. A knight of King Arthur's!"

"No wonder he disguised himself as a beggar," Philippa said. "I don't believe it! We saved a real knight!"

The repeated pounding of King Wallace's cup on the table gradually quieted the hall.

"Well, I must say, this is turning out differently than I envisioned. I don't know what to say, King Arthur. I'm afraid we almost hanged Sir Lancelot." With that statement, King Wallace sat down and put his head in his hands. "Oh my!"

"Sir Lancelot and I are both grateful that didn't occur. As to how he ended up here, I can only say that sometimes my knights seek solitude to strengthen their commitment to their vows. And this is where Sir Lancelot chose his solitude." He signaled for Lancelot to stand beside him.

"Now if I may, King Wallace, I would like to thank those responsible for saving Lancelot's life."

"Certainly, Your Majesty."

"Prince Gavin, please come forward." Arthur waited until Gavin stood before him. Unable to help himself, Gavin smiled at Sir Lancelot, who smiled in return.

"Prince Gavin, you are to be commended for your role in freeing Sir Lancelot and helping capture the real murderer and thief. It was your courage that allowed you to venture under cover into Manorbier Castle to learn the real identity and motivation of the murderer known as Dunham."

Several members of the crowd gasped at hearing his feat.

"It was a demonstration of your loyalty to a friend whom our world values so highly. Please kneel, Prince Gavin."

Gavin knelt before King Arthur. King Arthur pulled Excalibur from its sheath. Candlelight glinted off the brilliant sword. The crowd murmured.

Arthur held Excalibur above his head, and then slowly tapped the silver blade on Gavin's shoulders.

"Prince Gavin, I bestow upon you the title of Squire. You are hereby commanded to complete the first half of your training here at Pembroke Castle. Then, you will commence to Camelot to finish your training. At that point, you will be given the opportunity to attain your knighthood. Arise, Squire Gavin, and acknowledge your people's gratitude."

Gavin found himself unable to utter a word, but that didn't stop him from thrusting his arm into the air as a sign of victory. The enthusiastic display was so unusual for the young prince that the hall erupted in cheers. Gavin's mother put her hand on his father's shoulder. His brothers Robert and Sean shook their heads, but Gavin knew they were proud of him. He stood and stepped back, a wide grin still on his face.

"Bryan Balyard," King Arthur called.

Bryan rose and approached Arthur. He looked as unsteady as when Dunham had been forced to release him. Gavin tried to catch his eye, but Bryan focused on King Arthur.

"Of all honored today, you are the most unlikely hero. Your station in life was set. You were to be a blacksmith. However, the courage you showed when risking your life in hand-to-hand combat with a known murderer is courage that is needed in the protection of your country and its people."

Everyone sat in rapt silence as King Arthur continued to praise Bryan's bravery.

"There is only one type of person who possesses this type of courage. And that is a knight in my employ. I would like you to become one, if you will consent to leaving your apprenticeship with the blacksmith."

Bryan swayed and Gavin rushed to his side, but Lancelot stepped forward and shook Bryan's hand, steadying him. Beyond Bryan, James slapped his neighbor on the back and raised his mug in approval.

"You will commence to Camelot within the week to take your place with the Knights of the Round Table."

Bryan nodded.

"Kneel, Bryan Balyard." As King Arthur touched Bryan's shoulders with Excalibur, chills of joy ran through Gavin. He could think of no more fitting honor than that King Arthur had bestowed upon his friend. Arthur then handed Excalibur to Lancelot who tapped Bryan's shoulders with the famous sword, signaling his approval of his King's choice.

"Arise, Bryan Balyard, Knight-in-Training, and acknowledge your people's gratitude and the beginning of your service to King Arthur."

Bryan rose slowly, his face pale with disbelief. He returned to stand beside Gavin.

"A knight," he whispered.

Gavin took Bryan's hand and raised it in a salute to the hall. At the back of the room, Seanna stood. Their eyes met and with a nod of approval, she slipped out the door.

The hall quieted as King Arthur remained standing. "Princess Philippa."

With his newly-found brother's pride, Gavin greeted her with a thumbs up as she walked to Arthur.

"I have spoken of the courage you displayed that storm-tossed night on St. David's Head. To bestow another honor on top of that which you have already received might seem a trifle, but it is not. Your loyalty to Sir Lancelot, though you didn't know who he was, exemplified your respect for one you called a friend. For one man, one person to defend another, not knowing who that person may be, takes a courage few men have.

"Princess Philippa, I do hereby deem you a special friend of the court of Camelot. You will never be turned away or denied any favor you desire as long as Camelot stands!"

Philippa bowed and thanked King Arthur for the rare honor. Lancelot took her hand and raised it to his lips and her green eyes sparkled.

She returned to her seat. Gavin hugged her.

Bryan's face reddened when he imitated Lancelot and touched his lips to her hand.

Gavin grinned. *Might be some interesting times ahead.*

"Now, King Wallace," King Arthur said. "I suggest we let the celebration begin."

"Hear, hear!" King Wallace raised his goblet high.

"Hey, whataya think you're doin'?" A small voice made itself heard above the noise of the crowd. "Let me through. I got a right to be in 'ere."

18

AND THEN, TOM

King Wallace's knights parted to let a skinny urchin pass.

Gavin recognized the ragged white hair and laughed. He had told his father about Tom before the kings left for Manorbier, but nothing further had been said.

"Where is that king fella?"

The crowd murmured at his disrespect.

"I'm right up here, young fella," Arthur replied, chuckling.

"Well, it's 'bout time. I been waitin' out there for you to call for me." He walked up to King Arthur and bowed.

"Did you bring your things with you?" Arthur asked.

"Ever' thin' I own is right here." He patted his chest and smiled broadly. Then he saw Gavin.

"Prince Gavin." Tom bowed. "I thank you for not

forgettin' your promise to get me outta Manorbier Castle."

"You saved my life," Gavin said. "I wouldn't forget my promise."

"Squire Gavin," Arthur said, his sly smile warming Gavin's heart. "I present you with your Page-in-Training, Tom, uh..."

"Jist Tom, Sire."

"Just Tom, Squire Gavin."

Gavin grabbed Tom's bony hand and shook it, bringing a hardy laugh from the younger boy.

"King Wallace, I now give you back your hall," King Arthur said. Standing, King Wallace raised his cup and nodded to those seated at the table. Once they stood, he nodded to those in the hall and waited until they did the same.

"Let the mead flow in celebration of Squire Gavin, Sir Bryan, Princess Philippa, and Sir Lancelot!"

Tom left Gavin's side and grabbed a handful of King Wallace's shirt. Gavin laughed at the surprise on his father's face. He met his father's eyes and nodded.

King Wallace took hold of Tom's small hand and held it high. "And a cheer for Page-in-Training Tom!"

MORE ABOUT THE PLACES MENTIONED

All of the places mentioned in the story are real. If you have an opportunity to visit Wales, you can follow in the characters' footsteps just as I did in 2014.

Cardigan Bay: This is a huge bay on the western side of Wales. St. George's Channel funnels water from the Irish Sea into this inlet. It is surrounded by small cliffs, rolling grasslands, and sandy shores.

Manorbier Castle: The current stone castle sits at the edge of the village of Manorbier and dates from the 11th century. In the story, my castle is made of wood and would not have survived intact from the 400/500 AD. There is a Smuggler's Passage inside of the stone castle, and the castle itself sits on a cliff above the water. The castle is about 1/3 of the size of Pembroke Castle, home of Gavin, which may be one of the reasons King Edward wanted to take over King Wallace's Pembroke Castle.

Pembroke Castle: The current stone castle sits in the middle of the town of Pembroke. From the castle battlements you can see the growth that has grown up around the castle. This Pembroke Castle also dates from the 11th century. As with Manorbier, the original wooden castle would not have lasted. Pembroke is huge! It is located on a hill with a three-story rock wall on the side of the remaining moat. Every year the castle hosts a 2-day rock concert called Rock the Castle! Wonder what Gavin and friends would think of that!!

St. David's Head: Located on the outskirts of the town of St. David's, the Head sits above the waters of the Celtic Sea and the Irish Sea. You can climb to the top as in the story but today while you encounter wind and storms, you will also pass wild ponies grazing along the path. The Head is part of the Pembrokeshire Coastal Path, a popular hiking path.

ABOUT THE AUTHOR

A retired high school English teacher, Cheryl Carpinello now writes Tales &
Legends for Reluctant Readers, a cause dear to her heart. She uses her love
of the Legend of King Arthur to introduce young readers to this Timeless
Legend and to entice reluctant readers to read more. Her *Guinevere* trilogy
introduces young readers Guinevere and her friend Cedwyn as she struggles
with growing up and fulfilling her destiny as the future wife of King Arthur.

Cheryl also writes tales from Ancient Egypt, a favorite place of hers. *Sons of
the Sphinx* and *Tutankhamen Speaks* immerses readers in the magical and
dangerous world of Egypt 3000 years in the past.

She is also one of the Quest Authors. Her partners are Fiona Ingram from
the island of Cyprus and Wendy Leighton-Porter of Abu Dhabi. All three
authors take young readers on thrilling adventures through the ancient and
medieval worlds as well as current times.

Please connect with Cheryl at any of these sites:

www.cherylcarpinello.com
www.beyondtodayeducator.com
www.adventurequestbooks.com